WATERLESS MOUNTAIN

When they came to the prehistoric cliff-dwelling high in the rocks, they hurried by.

WATERLESS MOUNTAIN

By LAURA ADAMS ARMER

ILLUSTRATED BY
SIDNEY ARMER *and* LAURA ADAMS ARMER

DAVID McKAY COMPANY, INC.
NEW YORK

ARMER
WATERLESS MOUNTAIN

COPYRIGHT 1931
BY LONGMANS, GREEN AND CO.

COPYRIGHT RENEWED 1959
BY LAURA ADAMS ARMER

First Edition September 1931
Reprinted September 1931, November 1931, January 1932,
April 1932, January 1933, October 1934, April 1935, Oc-
tober 1936, April 1938, November 1939, November 1942,
December 1943, September 1946, January 1950, September
1952, November 1953, June 1955, October 1957, Septem-
ber 1959, September 1961, November 1963, August 1966,
February 1969, June 1972, March 1975, April 1977, No-
vember 1979, March 1981, December 1982, May 1984,
September 1985, October 1986

LIBRARY OF CONGRESS CATALOG CARD NUMBER: 77-75989
ISBN: 0-679-20233-1

PRINTED IN THE UNITED STATES OF AMERICA

FOREWORD

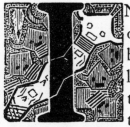N AUGUST 1924, my partner and I turned our two scraggly ponies and our treasured albino pack-horse loose in a corral at Oraibi and looked over the village. Hardly had we had time to buy a bottle of pop and roll a cigarette than we were informed that there was a lady artist in the schoolhouse, who had persuaded a Navaho medicine man to make a sacred sand-painting for her and, contrary to the ceremonial laws, leave it undestroyed for people to look at. Incredulous, we went to see. The lady received us with some restraint, our aspect did not seem to charm her. Still, she admitted us to her temporary studio, and there was the sand-painting, sure enough, complete even to the prayer-sticks around the edges, and many excellent pictures by herself to boot.

She grew more cordial after a while, and in talking with her about the Indians, we began to perceive the charm and sympathy which had won a medicine man to violate a dozen taboos for her. Finally she decided we were harmless. We invited her to our camp for a Navaho meal of goat's ribs, and she, game lady, accepted. So we went and got ready.

We looked at ourselves as we had not in some weeks, and

understood the coolness of our first reception — unshaven chins, the dust of the trail piled thick on filthy and tattered clothes, my partner's golden hair turned a dull brown, we were the sorriest looking pair of tramps you ever saw. We got ourselves clean, Mrs. Armer came and shared our rather crude victuals, and friendship began.

Partly because of her paintings of the Navaho legends, in which the Indians saw an unusual insight and an expression of many things which they did not expect white people to understand, partly because she has been guided in her contacts by one of the wisest and most sympathetic of all the Navahos' friends, and largely through her own personality, she has been able to come unusually close to these people in a very short time. Her knowledge of their real selves has enabled her to select a difficult theme for her book, the internal processes, the thoughts and feelings and growth of a Navaho boy who feels a vocation to become a medicine man. It is a daring subject for a white person to tackle, but within the limitations of a book for young people, Mrs. Armer has probably come as close to painting a true picture as anyone save a medicine man can do. Many readers will question the high religious ideas, the constant talk of beauty, the mysticism, that she ascribes to Younger Brother and his priestly Uncle; one can only say that, contrary to the general idea, many Indians are so.

February 1931

CONTENTS

"We Navahos call it the Waterless Mountain because on its top and on all of its sides there is not one spring; but no one knows what may be in its heart. There are six directions always—east, south, west, north, above and below. Below is the deep heart of things."

WATERLESS MOUNTAIN

CHAPTER I

THE FRIENDS OF YOUNGER BROTHER

N THE month of Short Corn, when drooping clouds floated white against the blue, and fringed dust rose from the washes, Younger Brother tended the sheep. They were homeward bound, for the sun was in the western sky. Younger Brother was only eight but he felt much older because he was alone with his mother's sheep. All day he had watched them and cared for the two little lambs who stayed so close to his side. No harm had come to them and soon he would have them safe in the corral under the sheltering cliffs.

Younger Brother was hungry. Already he could smell the coffee and the roasted mutton ribs that his mother was preparing inside the round mud house called the hogan.

He could see his father's pony tied to the juniper tree. His

father was a great silversmith. When he tired of making bracelets and rings, he rode about the desert to look after his cattle.

Younger Brother could remember sitting in the saddle in front
of his father. That was a long time ago, before he had a baby
sister. Now he was big enough to have a pony of his own but
he must herd the sheep so that his mother could have wool to
spin and weave, and mutton to cook. He would much rather
ride a pony as Elder Brother did.

Elder Brother wore his long hair in a knot because he was a
grown man. Uncle had given him his turquoise earrings,
which were family heirlooms. Uncle was Mother's brother and
he was a medicine man. He told stories in the winter time
while everyone sat around the fire in the middle of the hogan.

Younger Brother liked the winter time with its stories and its
pine nuts, but he liked the month of Short Corn too, when the
lambs were strong and jumpy, and the baby cottontails hid
under the sagebrush. He liked every month and every day,
and he liked to get home with his mother's sheep.

"Yego, hurry!" he called, as he threw a rattling can of
pebbles toward the flock.

Mother met him at the corral and helped him put up the
bars. Then they entered the hogan for supper.

Baby Sister greeted them with a laugh. Like all other
Navaho babies she was tied tightly in her cradle which was just
a board. The tie strings which criss-crossed in front were like
the lightning. The bow to hold the canopy was like the rainbow and the fringe on the side was like the rain.

Baby's arms and hands were wrapped inside the blanket and

she couldn't move her body on the board. She could only move her head from side to side, but she was happy and content until she saw Brother eating. She too was hungry and she cried so loudly that Mother untied her and gave her a mutton rib all juicy and sizzly from the fire.

When darkness came everyone lay down on his own sheepskin and fell asleep. That night Younger Brother had a dream. It was about the Yay. Yay is the Navaho word for a god or holy being. Younger Brother dreamed of the first time he saw a Yay. That was in the month of Slender Wind, when his Uncle had given a sing, or healing ceremony, for Mr. Many Goats.

On the eighth day of the ceremony twenty boys and girls were to be initiated. They sat on the ground in a semi-circle, with their backs to the north. All the boys were naked but the girls were dressed in their very best velveteen jackets fastened with silver buttons. Strings of turquoise and coral hung about their necks.

The children had been told to sit quietly with bowed heads and wait for the Yays to come. Some of the girls had their mothers beside them but the boys were alone and trying not to be afraid. Younger Brother heard the cry, "Wu hu, wu hu !"

Looking up he saw the holy one with naked body all dazzling white and with a mask of deerskin over his face. The Yay's long black hair fell over his painted white shoulders and a fox skin hung from his silver-girt waist.

Younger Brother was told to stand while pollen was sprinkled over his body. After that he was struck with two long yucca leaves. He was not afraid. He did not cry a bit. He was feeling queer. He had never felt like that before. It seemed as if the whole world were whirling light and warmth. He could feel life gliding over him in warm waves.

He laughed without making any noise. He could smell fresh green things growing, though there was nothing but dry sagebrush about him. He could hear the song of the mocking-bird and of Doli the bluebird. He could hear the notes tumbling and pouring over one another, though there was not a bird around. He could see colors shimmering about the white body of the Yay. He even felt as if his feet left the ground and he were lifted up into the air.

In his dream of this initiation, Younger Brother lived his ecstasy over again. He knew that, like the Navaho boy who was given wings, he could fly right up to the sky, and he did.

He played with the Star Children. They were lovely children dressed in brilliant sharp stones of blue and white and black and yellow. They sparkled from their own light and when they laughed, little specks of star-dust shook from their finger tips and toes. They carried bows and arrows. Sometimes they sent a shaft flying into the dark, and people of the earth said, "There is a shooting star."

Just as Younger Brother dreamed of the shooting star he awoke. Everything in the hogan was still but through the smoke hole in the roof came the sound that star-dust makes when it falls to earth. Younger Brother looking up, whispered, "Big Star, I am your child, for I have heard your song."

After that night of dreaming, Younger Brother noticed that many more wonderful things happened, even in the daytime when he was alone with the sheep. If a whirlwind came twisting toward him he sat very still and said, "Wind, I am your child, for your trail is marked on the ends of my fingers."

It was the same with the clouds that he watched. They were living beings to him. He ran races with cloud shadows that purpled the mesas, and laughing he called, "Cloud, I am your child, for you have poured water in the rocks for me."

He loved the rainbow best of all, for when it came to watch over the month of Short Corn, it stretched its beauty to the month of Tall Corn. Younger Brother, sitting in the shade of the tasseled corn, spoke to the Rainbow People:

"Rainbow, I am your child, for you have brought the rain to the parched earth and the corn is green."

When the thunder spoke, Younger Brother was silent, for he felt very small then and wished he were home with his mother, her child in her arms.

One day when his mother had finished weaving a rug, she packed it with a sheep pelt on the back of a burro. She lifted Younger Brother up in front of the load and they started down the canyon to visit the trader.

Younger Brother had never been to a trading post. He had never seen a white person in all his eight years. Mother walked, leading the burro. The sun shone on the yellow cliffs and the shadows fell in welcome strips of coolness across the sandy wash.

Younger Brother was happy and excited for he was to see

strange sights. Mother would know what to do. Mile after mile they traveled in the sand, sometimes passing little peach orchards on the edge of the wash.

When they came to the prehistoric cliff dwellings high up in the rocks, they hurried by, for the holy people live there and it is not well for the people of the earth to disturb them. Younger Brother was glad every time they were safely past.

The sun was almost overhead and Younger Brother was thirsty. He could see no water about, but he told Mother he must have some. She went to the edge of the cliff and dug a little hole in the sand with her hands. In a few moments it was filled with water that seeped in from below the dry sand. Mother always knew what to do.

It seemed a long time before they reached the trading post, but just as Younger Brother was thinking they never would arrive, they turned a bend in the canyon.

There at the base of a rocky hill stood a group of houses, different from any the boy had ever seen. They were not round like a hogan nor were they made of logs and mud. To Younger Brother they seemed huge and reminded him of the cliff dwellings.

He was frightened. Maybe the white people who lived there were like the holy people of the cliffs. Mother wasn't afraid. He could tell because she was lifting him to the ground and tying the burro near a Navaho wagon loaded with sacks of wool. It must be all right.

Mother went straight into the store with her blanket and sheep pelt. Younger Brother clung to her skirt. When he dared to look up he saw row after row of canned peaches and tomatoes piled on shelves to the ceiling. Lower down there were rolls of bright calico and velveteen and plush. This must be some kind of magic house to hold so many beautiful things that people liked.

Mother walked through the store and opened another door. There in a very small room sat a very big man. He did not sit on the floor as Navaho men did. His feet only were on the floor and he sat up in the air on a board supported by four sticks. Another wide board on higher sticks stood in front of him, and the Big Man made queer clicking noises on rows of little round white things that he pressed down with his fingers. The fingers worked rapidly and surely, like the feet of the Yays when they dance in a ceremony.

The Big Man did not look up nor say a word. He continued to press the little round white things as if his life depended on them. After a while, out of the object he was punching, he pulled a piece of white paper covered with small black marks.

Looking up he saw Mother. He smiled and held her hand.

She said, "Grandfather," not that he was old, but because that is a term of respect among Navahos.

Then the Big Man patted Younger Brother on the head and said in Navaho, "Grandchild."

Younger Brother thought he had never seen so kind a face and he knew right away that the Big Man must be a medicine man. He could feel power shining through the blue eyes, and tingling in the fingers that touched his head.

He thought how comfortable it would be to stay near the

Big Man with the kind voice.   He hoped Mother would bring him to the trading post every time she had a blanket to sell.

The Big Man had only said "Grandchild" and patted him on the head but Younger Brother knew that, like the stars, the clouds, the rainbow and the dawn, this man was his friend.

CHAPTER II

YELLOW BEAK

HEN Younger Brother and Mother reached home again late in the evening, all the family awaited them. Baby Sister was creeping on the floor and playing with the gray tiger cat. She waved her hands and laughed when she saw Mother. Everyone wanted to see what Mother had brought from the store. Of course there would be sugar and flour and coffee and maybe there would be canned peaches.

Sure enough there were canned peaches and a can of strawberry jam. Mother was surprised to find the jam because she had not traded for it. The Big Man must have put it in for a present. Younger Brother was sure it was meant for him because the Big Man had called him Grandchild.

Every time Younger Brother became acquainted with people they gave him something to remember them by. The Star Children had shaken star-dust to him. The Cloud People had poured water for him. The Earth Mother had given him corn to eat and now the Big Man with the smile had given him strawberry jam. He would keep the colored picture that was on the can. He put it inside his shirt while no one was looking.

Mother saved the jam for breakfast and next morning, which was warm and sunny, everyone sat outside the hogan to eat. The coffee boiling on the campfire added new sweetness to the desert air.

The lambs skipped over the rocks and bees buzzed about the sagebrush. The lone cottonwood tree harbored a host of little birds and one mocking-bird sang as loud as he could, in imitation of all the other bird people. It was a morning when everything sang a song.

Younger Brother strolled toward the corral, still eating his strawberry jam. There was jam on his bread, on his little brown fingers and all around his lips. The bees were attracted to it. They thought it was some new kind of sweet red flower. They settled on the edge of the bread and began to eat their breakfast.

Younger Brother stood still to watch them. He did not brush them away and soon they were crawling on his hands and one even lit on his sweet red lips and ate to his heart's content. When they were through he said to them:

"The Big Man sent it to us. He is our friend."

So while the sweet cedar smoke rose to greet the morning sky and while the birds sang and the bees buzzed, Younger Brother let down the bars of the corral and all the sheep ran out, ready to start on the daily hunt for grass.

Mother was boiling water on the campfire for the red dye she had brought from the post. Already she had shrunk her white yarn in the hot water and had wound it round and round the outside of the hogan to dry. Because she shrunk the yarn she spun, the finished rug kept its shape when it was washed. Mother made the best rugs of all the women.

Father was melting Mexican silver dollars in a clay crucible and pouring the molten metal into a mold chiseled out of sandstone. He had greased the mold with mutton tallow before pouring in the molten silver. He was making a bracelet for Younger Brother. It was to have a very blue turquoise set in the middle with butterflies engraved on each side of the stone. Father was a very great silversmith.

Elder Brother had gone rabbit hunting and Younger Brother must be off with the sheep. Every day he had to travel further from home because, little by little, the grass was disappearing before the hungry sheep. The little shepherd went higher up the canyon than he had ever been before.

He reached the place of crooked rocks where the crooked stone people sat around in circles. They sat around a stone fire with stone flames and everything was quiet. Younger Brother knew that some of the huge crooked rocks had once been giants, who went about the country destroying people.

He had heard about the two splendid children of the Sun Bearer, who had come to earth to save the Navahos from the wicked giants. He knew how the Sun Bearer had given weapons of lightning to his sons and how they had hurled thunderbolts at the giants to slay them.

Younger Brother was most respectful to the crooked rocks. He let the sheep graze at their base but he wouldn't think of climbing on a lone rock himself. He watched the birds fly about them and he wondered if there were any eagle nests resting in the arms of the quiet stone giants.

He knew that the Eagle People lived somewhere in the deep blue, high above the people of the earth. He was respectful to the eagles also because he knew they could look down on him and see everything he did. He was extremely respectful in his thought of the Eagle People, who seemed as mighty as the sun that was shining so ardently on the strange weird forms of the stone giants.

While the sheep lazily grazed in the noontime, Younger Brother rested in the shade of the rocks. He could hear the wind singing in the canyon. The Wind People were always kindly in the summer time. They played with tumbleweeds, rolling them over and over and making them hide in the little hollows at the base of the cliffs. They danced in spirals in the sunshine and sometimes they lifted the red band off of Younger Brother's head and waved it to the tumbleweeds.

The little boy felt very lazy lying on the ground with his hands behind his head. He felt dreamy and drowsy while the wind murmured in the canyon. He listened to its song and soon he seemed to hear the words:

"Look up, Grandchild, look up, Grandchild."

He looked up, way, way up to the crest of the strange rocks and there he saw Yellow Beak, the eagle. He had ridden the sun rays from out of the far blue and was resting on top of one of the rocks. He was as still as the rocks themselves. Everything was still. The wind stopped singing, the tumbleweeds lay quiet, and even the sheep were motionless before the majesty of Yellow Beak.

He did not move a feather. He just looked down at Younger Brother with his strong eagle eyes which could look straight at the sun without blinking.

Younger Brother was very still too, looking up, looking up. He felt small and earthbound and respectful, oh, so very respectful. He was not afraid of Yellow Beak, and he was not wishing for Mother as he did when the thunder spoke. He was just looking up and Yellow Beak was looking down, but both of them knew that something was happening.

Younger Brother remembered that his people set traps baited with rabbits, for the eagles. He knew that when a Navaho trapped an eagle, he never killed him, but took his tail feathers and soft downy feathers and let him fly away.

Medicine men needed the feathers to put around the pictures of the sun and on the mask of the dawn god. Younger Brother knew that the medicine men must have eagle feathers but he wished eagles did not have to be trapped.

He hoped no one would ever trap Yellow Beak who was looking down on him and making him understand things the way the stars did, the way the rainbow did and the way the Big Man did when he smiled.

Just as he was wishing and hoping for the freedom of the eagles, dazzling light and color streamed down from the sky. Yellow Beak slowly lifted his wings and mounted the sun rays. He gave a glad call from the deep blue, waved his wings to Younger Brother and was soon lost to sight.

Slowly in the warm light something fluttered from the heights. It came nearer and nearer and fell at Younger Brother's feet. He picked it up and held it to his heart. It was a tail feather Yellow Beak had sent to him. He held it to his lips and breathed on it four times, then he hid it in his shirt. He would care for it some way. He would not let anyone know what happened; not even Mother nor Uncle — not yet.

The feather had come to him right out of the sky. Yellow Beak had sent it to him on a ray of light. More would come when he needed them. He knew they would always come when he needed them, for Yellow Beak was his friend.

CHAPTER III

SPRING POLLEN

LDER BROTHER riding his pony up from the wash had lost patience with the burro he was trying to drive ahead of him. He whacked the animal with a stick but it stood stubbornly immovable halfway up the bank. The two water kegs slung on each side of it were full of muddy alkaline water from the spring. The burro objected to climbing the steep bank. Elder Brother had coaxed and prodded with his stick till his temper was bad. He cried wrathfully, "You child of a snake ! You castout of poverty ! Move, move !"

The burro did not move. He only waved one long ear disdainfully. Elder Brother was desperate. He disliked the task of hauling the water. It was beneath his dignity. Again he belabored the burro. Again he swore, "Blockhead from the land of hunger ! I will fix you. I will make you move."

Veering his pony he rode back to the spring, where a stunted juniper grew in the rocks. He picked some leaves and chewed them carefully and deliberately. Then he rode in front of the stubborn burro and with great solemnity spat the juice of the juniper in the burro's face.

The animal swerved and some loosened rock rolling down the bank, splashed in the shallow stream. The burro's uncertain footing gave him no choice. He moved forward.

Elder Brother's anger gradually faded away and riding through the sagebrush, he experienced the calm which is born of faith. He had never known the juniper to fail.

It was only a mile back to camp. Up by the red sandstone cliff he could see his little brother coming with the sheep. He waved his hand to him, and when within speaking distance said, "Juice of the juniper adds speed to the legs. Our people are wise in their teachings. If a thing will not go, spit the juice of the juniper in its face."

"What will happen then ?" Younger Brother asked.

"It will go, it will move. Remember, juice of the juniper is strong magic for motion."

"I shall remember," said the little boy, as he looked at his handsome brother with pride and admiration. He thought he was almost as wise as Uncle. He would remember about the juniper.

After the two boys reached home and their chores were done for the day, the little boy ran to a cave not far from the hogan. Here it was that he kept his treasures. Not that he had many, but they were very precious.

There was no place in the hogan to keep things. If Mother took off her turquoise necklace, she dug a little hole in the sand floor, put the beads in and covered them with her own special sheepskin.

No one would think of touching Mother's turquoise, but Younger Brother would never leave his treasures where anyone could find them. First of all no one would know they were treasures. That was the worst of it.

To reach his secret cave in a cliff, it was necessary to climb to the top of a boulder. From it he could just reach the floor of the cave whose opening was so small, he could only enter by lying on his stomach and wriggling in. After he was in he could sit up without bumping his head and reach back to a little ledge where he kept his treasures.

He was very happy thinking of his new prize. He said to himself, "Today my heap will welcome a great one."

He took the red bandana off of his hair and smoothed it out on the floor of the cave. Then from his shirt he took the eagle feather Yellow Beak had sent from the blue. Carefully he wrapped it in the red bandana. Lovingly he lifted it to his lips and blew on it four times, before he placed it on the little ledge at the back of the cave. He put a rock on it to hold it safely.

This was a very important ceremony for Younger Brother. He was thinking of Yellow Beak, his new strong friend, who lived somewhere in the sky beyond the reach of human eyes.

He thought of all his friends. He had keepsakes from all of them. From the Star Children he had bits of sparkling mica. From the Wind he had four little pieces of petrified wood.

They were of four different colors. One was white, one was gray-blue, one was yellow and one was black.

Younger Brother kept the white piece on the east side of the cave, the blue on the south, the yellow on the west, the black on the north side. This was very necessary because those are the right colors for the four cardinal points. Uncle had told him about the colors and he had never forgotten.

He liked his little pieces of petrified wood because the strong wind had uncovered them in the sand for him, and besides they were smooth and such beautiful colors.

Perhaps he liked best of all his stones, the one the Red Ant People had given him. It was a dark red garnet that he could look through. The Red Ants were rather a fearful people. Most Navahos stayed away from ant hills for very good reasons of their own. Younger Brother knew these reasons and he never walked too close to an ant hill.

One day a little lamb who was weak and tired from the hot sunshine, fell right down on an ant hill. Younger Brother ran to pick him up. He carried the tired little lamb to its mother. When he put it on the ground he found the beautiful red stone stuck in the wool of the lamb's back. The Ant People had put it there. They had brought it up from the underworld with all the other gravel.

Younger Brother had never told anyone about that, because his people were afraid of ants, but he knew the ants wanted the little lamb to have the red stone, so he kept it along with his other treasures in the cave.

And what do you think he kept it in ? A little pottery bowl !

He had found that bowl in the sand after a big rain. His friends, the clouds sent that and it had cloud patterns drawn with black on its beautiful white surface.

His friends were so kind to him he liked to think of them all. He remembered the good strawberry jam, that the Big Man had given to him. He looked at the paper he had saved from the can. It had red-colored mountains painted on it. At least he thought they were mountains. Maybe they were ant hills. He had never seen a fresh strawberry, so how was he to know they were strawberries on the paper? That was the best keepsake he had so far from the Big Man and he put it in the little pottery bowl of the clouds.

As he sat in his treasure cave he could look out on the eastern sky. It was colored like the red stone when he held it to the sun. He thought the whole earth might be a red stone for the sun to look through just before it set in the west. Probably it was. He couldn't see any reason why it shouldn't be. The sky at noon was a big turquoise bowl. He knew that, and at night it was the darkness stone of jet, set all over with shining stars.

Younger Brother wondered if Father had finished the bracelet yet. He would go back to the hogan and see. That was to be his keepsake from Father and from the blue sky because the turquoise belonged to the sky.

By the time he reached the hogan the sun had finished looking through the ruby-red earth and everything was gray.

It was good to be inside for supper. Mother had made a fine

rabbit stew and the corn cakes he liked so well. The cakes were baked in the Dutch oven that came from the trading post.

After supper Father tried the bracelet on Younger Brother's wrist. It was perfect and everybody was happy. Father knew how to make such beautiful things with his hands. He couldn't tell stories the way Uncle did but his silver work made the boy think of moonlight on the mesas.

Younger Brother fell asleep early, holding one hand over his new bracelet and holding in his mind all the beautiful secrets of the day.

The next morning was lovelier than the last and everyone lingered long about the breakfast fire. Father, having finished the bracelet, felt like doing nothing in particular. Mother was in no hurry to weave. She smiled at Baby Sister playing in the sand. Elder Brother thought he might ride to the post. He needed more cartridges for his rifle.

Only Younger Brother must be busy because the sheep were already bleating to be out of the corral. He didn't mind because he might have some more adventures. Even if he didn't it would be all right because he had so much to think about.

Just to watch the sheep grazing made him think about the grass and how it grew after the rain. He thought of its roots underground. He thought of seeds underground, waiting in the darkness for the rain to moisten them and swell them so they could burst into leaves and roots.

Surely growing things were magical. They liked water to drink the same as people did. He wondered what they ate. Probably deep in the ground all the roots had their food. It

The Bumble Bee put his feet down in pollen.

was fun to think of all the little roots of plants sitting around eating dinner. Plants did not walk the way people did but some plants tried to. There was the squash vine. It tried to travel.

Two things he had noticed — everything on the earth grew upward toward the sun and things under the earth grew downward toward the water. He had heard about the Under-Water People, like the fish and the snakes.

While Younger Brother thought about these mysteries of the earth, he drove the sheep up a trail on the mesa. They were nearly to the top and had found extra good grass among the bushes. Younger Brother noticed that things were beginning to bloom. Butterfly lilies and red feather flowers were looking at him.

A big bumble bee, all yellow with pollen, flew out of a lily. Younger Brother wondered if the Bumble Bee People gathered the pollen for ceremonies the way the Navahos do. He watched the bumble bee go to another flower.

He put his feet down in pollen. He put his hands down in pollen. He put his head down in pollen. He was enacting the magic formula the Spider Woman gave the Children of the Sun. Younger Brother was much interested and he found himself saying to the bumble bee:

"Your feet are pollen, your hands are pollen, your body is pollen, your mind is pollen, your voice is pollen. The trail is beautiful, be still."

No sooner had he finished saying this than the bumble bee flew right onto the top of his head. Younger Brother held perfectly still wondering what was happening. The bumble bee had put his feet down with pollen on the boy's black hair. He had walked right around in a circle and then flown away bumbling.

Younger Brother wondered why he felt so extra happy that day. He didn't know there was a golden ring of pollen on his head. Only the Sky People looking down could see that.

The birds sang more sweetly as they flew over him. Every living thing seemed wrapped in peace. Bright-colored butter-flies spread their wings over the lilies.

Younger Brother held his new bracelet up to the sky to see how it matched his turquoise. They were so near of a color he thought it must be a piece of sky that was set in the silver.

The Sun Bearer traveling to the west saw the little hand lifted toward him and he said with joy:

"Surely the children of the earth are restored in beauty."

CHAPTER IV

A NEW SONG

OUNGER BROTHER and Uncle had succeeded in rounding up the horses. The Big Man from the trading post was expected in a few days to look them over and choose what he wanted. The next task was to find the steers. The little Navaho boy had been excused from herding the sheep so that he could help Uncle. They were riding their ponies up a narrow rocky gorge and keeping a sharp lookout for the red-and-white yearling that was missing. Tracks led to the water hole. There in the damp sand beside the water, new tracks were found, tracks of the mountain lion. Uncle said:

"The Soft-footed Chief has been hunting. He is a good hunter and grows fat on our cattle."

Younger Brother hoped his yearling had not helped to fatten the Soft-footed Chief. Uncle had given it to him when it was just a little calf. He had watched it grow and was proud of his possession. He asked Uncle if they were to hunt the mountain lion.

"No, my child. He is one of the pets the Turquoise Woman gave to our people. It is better that we leave him to follow his own trail of beauty."

"Uncle, where does the Turquoise Woman live?"

"On an island in the wide water of the west. There she waits every day in her turquoise house for her husband, who carries the sun."

"And when the Sun Bearer reaches his home in the west, what does he do with the sun, Uncle?"

"He hangs it up on a turquoise peg on the turquoise wall of the turquoise house of the Turquoise Woman. It goes *Tla, tla, tla, tla,* as it sways on the wall. When it is still, the Sun Bearer, resting on the floor, lights his pipe from its fire. He cannot rest too long, for every morning he must start across the sky from the east, bearing the sun on his left shoulder."

"I should like to go to the wide water of the west, Uncle. I should like to see the turquoise house and the Turquoise Woman."

The two talked as they rode. They were following a narrow stream of water that traced its way under the tender green lacery of alders. The trail their ponies followed was narrow and overgrown. Sometimes Younger Brother wondered if it were a trail, it was so full of loose rocks.

He was glad Uncle had let him ride with him. Uncle was a medicine man who knew the stories of the Holy People who lived in the land before the Navahos came. They were the people who built their dwellings in caves high up in the cliffs. They must have been a busy people, to judge from all the broken bits of pottery scattered about the country. The old pots were painted with black on white or red, and the designs were strange to the Navahos. Sometimes the Navaho mothers copied the designs in their weavings.

Uncle had told Younger Brother many stories of the ancient people and he knew about the boy who wanted to find a new song. He knew how the boy had traveled on a rainbow to reach the House of Dawn. Younger Brother had seen the House of Dawn and the House of Evening Twilight, high in a canyon wall — so high that everyone knew they could be reached only by a rainbow trail.

Younger Brother wondered if there were any stone houses of the ancient ones near where they were riding. Uncle had never before been so far up the canyon. Maybe no one had. It was very wild. The trail had given out and they were forced to ride up hill through brush and over loose rocks. They were still looking for the lost cattle.

Breaking through the brush, they came unexpectedly to a clear space. There, at the foot of a cliff, they found a spring of water. It fed the stream they had been following. Younger Brother could hardly believe his eyes when he saw his own red-and-white yearling drinking at the spring.

"Uncle," he whispered, "the Soft-footed Chief did not kill my yearling."

"It is well, my child. I will rope him and we will lead him home to the corral."

While Uncle roped the yearling, Younger Brother rode around the end of the cliff. He liked this country with its rocks and mountains and trees. He felt light within, the way he had at the initiation. He thought he too would like to make a new song.

Suddenly the stillness of the mountains was broken by a queer sound like the rattling of hoofs on stone. Looking in the direction of the sound, Younger Brother saw a tremendous round cave in the mountainside, filled with many little stone houses enveloped in blue shadow.

Younger Brother still heard the clattering, rattling noise, and then into a streak of sunshine on the floor of the cave leapt seven slender deer. Just for a moment they paused in the light and then they leapt and danced on the stone floor and were lost to sight in the shrubbery in front of the cave.

Everything was again still except Younger Brother's heart. That was beating wildly and words were pounding in his head for release. He knew he had found a new song and the words poured out of him like the song of the bluebirds. This is what he sang:

> *In the yellow sun they danced,*
> *Slender Horns and Slender Feet.*
> *Near their shadowed homes they danced,*
> *Slender Horns and Slender Feet.*

Then he rode back to Uncle and whispered:
"The Deer People ! I saw them enter their houses."

Uncle looked at the child. His big brown eyes were opened wide. He was breathing fast and trembling. Uncle knew something had happened. Probably the boy had been blessed

They leapt and danced on the stone floor.

with a vision. That was good. He would make a powerful medicine man if he had visions. He spoke to him.

"It is well, my child. We will return to the hogan. To-night you may tell us all about the Deer People."

Riding back and leading the red-and-white yearling, Younger Brother was very quiet. He knew he had seen the dwellings of the ancients. That night in the hogan by the fire he sang his new song for Uncle, who said:

"It is a new song. Never have I heard it before. Now you must have a new name. I shall call you Little Singer and because the Deer People danced for you, I shall teach you their songs. It will take many years to learn them. Not until you are a man will you know them all, but we shall begin in four days."

Nobody believed that Younger Brother had seen a real cave with real houses. Only the Big Man believed because he knew that anything magic or wonderful could exist and did exist in Navaho land. Besides he had a photograph of the big cave with all the houses. He had never shown it to anyone because he too liked to watch the Deer People dance in the sunlight and he knew they never would if noisy people went to their homes with guns and canned goods. So he and Younger Brother kept the secret together.

CHAPTER V

A FRIEND IN NEED

UT GRANDFATHER, I cannot pay for the wire."

"Why not, my child ? Did I not pay six pesos for your corn ?"

"But Grandfather, I am poor. A little mouse chewed a hole in my wife's moccasin."

The Big Man looked up from his desk in astonishment. What excuse would these Navahos make next ?

"The little mouse chewed a hole in your wife's moccasin, and then what happened ?"

"I had to pay a medicine man to sing for her. That was very bad luck to have a mouse eat a moccasin."

"It certainly was bad luck, Hasteen — bad luck for every-body."

"So you see, Grandfather, I cannot pay for the wire."

The Navaho was very serious. He had driven fifteen miles with the corn and he must take back the barbed wire to protect his field. His wife was with him and she had a rug to sell. The trader weighed it and paid her in cash. She had intended to redeem her turquoise bracelet which had been pawned in the winter, but if her husband needed the wire, the money must go for that.   She handed it to the Big Man, saying:

"Is there enough to buy coffee and sugar, too ?"

"No," he answered.   "There is not enough."

"When do you buy the cattle, Grandfather ?" the Navaho asked.

"Tomorrow I start.   I go up the wash first."

"I have only two steers, Grandfather.   Will you look at them tomorrow ?"

"When tomorrow comes I can tell."

When tomorrow came the Big Man drove up the wash in his car.   He sang scraps of songs, when he wasn't smoking a cigar. They were old-fashioned songs like:

> *Say darling say,*
> *When I'm far away,*
> *Sometimes you may*
> *Think of me, dear.*

Sometimes he would break into a Navaho song, which sounded like the howl of a coyote.   He drove fast, but the wheel obeyed a steady hand and a clear head.   Near a clump of cedars he stopped to speak to a young Navaho who was trying to catch his saddle horse.

"I will help you, son."   With his machine he headed the horse toward its owner, who grabbed the bridle and mounted. The young man rode to the side of the Big Man's car and said:

"Grandfather, I need a dollar, for I am hungry."

The Big Man handed him a dollar. The Navaho took it and, with a winning smile, said:

"I am sorry I did not ask for two dollars, Grandfather."

The Big Man laughed and said, "I would not have given you two, my boy." Then he drove on, smiling at the ways of these brown people, whom he loved.

At the camp where Younger Brother's family lived, Mother had been dyeing her wool. Yarn and bunches of uncarded wool were drying on the rocks.

Some of the red dye had been left and Younger Brother had dipped a half-grown sheep in it. He had done it to make Baby Sister laugh, and they were both laughing as the Big Man's car appeared from behind the rocks that sheltered their camp.

The pink mottled sheep stood stupidly staring at the car, while Younger Brother grabbed Sister and ran into the hogan. He had never before seen an automobile go. He had seen this one parked at the trading post, but this was the first time the Big Man had visited their home.

Younger Brother called excitedly to Mother:

"The Big Man! He comes in the wagon without horses."

The trader joined the family inside the hogan, where they all sat on the floor, graciously hospitable. Mother left her loom to stir the fire and make fresh coffee.

"I could eat mutton, Sister," said the Big Man.

Mother put some ribs on the coals to roast, while Father talked to the guest. They did not immediately talk of buying and selling. It is not Navaho etiquette to plunge at once into the business of the day.

Younger Brother sat very quietly watching the Big Man as he talked. This was the second time he had seen him and he liked him just as well as before.

After everyone had eaten mutton ribs and fried bread, the Big Man went outside to his car and brought in a flour sack filled with apples, sweet crackers and tobacco. He gave the tobacco to Father and the sweet crackers to Mother. Then he handed an apple to Younger Brother and smiled. He always smiled when he gave something.

Because Younger Brother was so shy, he could say nothing. He only looked up at the Big Man the way he had looked up at Yellow Beak. The smile made him sure of his friend.

While he ate the apple the men went out to look at the cattle. The Big Man chose what he wanted and told Father to drive them to the post in a week. After shaking hands with everyone he stepped into his car. He must be off to the next camp to look at the two steers of the mouse and moccasin man.

To his surprise his car wouldn't start. "Some engine trouble," he thought as he got out to lift the hood. He could find nothing wrong, but for ten precious minutes he worked and could not start the engine.

Younger Brother watched every motion. He knew the Big Man was worried. He was not smiling. The little boy thought very hard. A friend should help a friend. The Big Man could not start his car. Like a flash the child remembered what Elder Brother had told him. "If a thing will not go, spit the juice of the juniper in its face."

Without a moment's hesitation he ran to the tree where

Father always tied his horse.   He chewed a sprig of juniper and when he had a good mouthful of the juice, he boldly went in front of the radiator and spat at it.   Immediately the engine turned over.

Everyone was amazed.   No one knew what had happened. The Big Man said, "It's always that way with a car.   When you do all the right things it balks, and then all of a sudden when it gets ready, it goes."

Younger Brother didn't say a word but he knew he had proven the magical power of juniper juice.   The car buzzed out of sight and Younger Brother felt so gay he chased the pink mottled sheep over a hill and back again.

Baby Sister, who could walk a little, laughed so hard she fell right down in the sand just as Brother and the pink sheep reached the hogan.   Mother picked her up and laughed too.

Soon everyone was laughing and no one knew how it had all started.   Even the pink sheep laughed "Baa, baa, baa, baa." The burro joined in with his "He haw" and a blue jay in the juniper just screamed at the top of his voice.   It all came about through the spitting of juniper juice and that surely was enough to make anyone laugh.

CHAPTER VI

THE FIRST SPINNER

HE GRAY tiger cat lay stretched in the sun-shine on top of Mother's hogan. He was asleep but he must have been dreaming about something, for every once in a while his whiskers would twitch or the black end of his striped tail would shake a little. Maybe he was dreaming about Baby Sister and the fork she tried to jab into him before he jumped on top of the hogan for safety.

Maybe he was dreaming about the big spider he had seen when he went hunting for field mice. That spider had a house in the ground with a hinged door. Tiger Cat had never seen such a big spider. Not being a Navaho, the cat didn't know that the Spider Woman was very kindly toward the First People.

Uncle knew that. He had told Younger Brother a beautiful story about First Man and First Woman when they sat singing by their spring of water.

First Man sat on one side of the spring and First Woman

33

faced him on the opposite side. They were singing because they were happy to have such good water.

One day First Man noticed what he thought was a beautiful piece of fruit in the middle of his spring. He wanted it but couldn't reach it so he asked the Spider Woman, whom he knew, what she could do about getting it for him.

"I can spin a web across the spring," she said.

"All right. Do it, Spider Woman," said First Man.

So she spun a very beautiful, strong web over the water and walked out on it. When she reached the place where the supposed fruit lay, she found that it was a big shining, white shell. She took it to First Man and it made him happy to have it.

For the next three days the Spider Woman was asked to spin her web and walk to the middle of the spring.

On the second day she brought back a big piece of turquoise, on the third day she found an abalone shell, and on the fourth day, the black stone.

First Man was much pleased. First Woman said, "I wish I could spin and weave."

So Spider Woman taught her how to do those two useful things. She taught her daughters and ever since then, Navaho women have known how.

Mother was weaving under the summer shelter while the gray tiger cat dreamed and twitched on the roof.

Lambs played about Mother's loom and one of them tried to chew a ball of yarn. Baby Sister decided that, as she couldn't reach the cat, she would try her fork on a lamb. Babies never think about hurting things. They just naturally kick and cry or laugh, without regard for grown-ups or pets.

Mother thought that whatever Baby Sister did was cute and she never scolded her. It had been the same way with Younger Brother when he was a baby, and with Elder Brother, too though that was so long ago Mother had forgotten.

Elder Brother was making a pair of new buckskin moccasins. Mother had colored the white skin with a mixture of alder bark, mountain mahogany and cedar ashes. She had dipped two corn-cobs in the liquid and beaten the leather with them for hours.

Elder Brother had cowhide soles all ready to sew on to the buckskin, and enough silver dimes with copper stems, to make a row right up the outside of each moccasin.

It was hard work to sew with rawhide. He had to make holes in the leather with a sharp awl. He was patient because he liked to dress well. He was very proud inside, about himself. Of course he didn't know what he looked like as there were no mirrors in the land but he felt handsome, especially when he rode out on his pony to hunt for rabbits and prairie dogs.

Once he took Younger Brother hunting and they tried using an old-fashioned bow and arrow. Uncle had made them. Not many Navahos can do that.

While the family sat working in the shade of the cedar bough shelter, Younger Brother came home with the sheep. He was glad to have some corn bread. He said he had been far that day and had seen a rattlesnake sunning itself on a rock.

"What did you do when you saw him ?" asked Elder Brother.

"Nothing but run away. What should I do ? I wouldn't bother him because Uncle says that snakes were Navahos at one time. Uncle says to be respectful to snakes always."

"I have never killed one myself," said Elder Brother.

"If you did, Uncle would have to sing the Lightning Chant for you. That drives away all the evil things that strike and sting."

"I shall not kill a snake," said the big brother. "I shall let him crawl as he pleases."

CHAPTER VII

THE YOUNG DAUGHTER OF HASTEEN SANI

ASTEEN SANI was a good friend and neighbor of Younger Brother's family. He lived two miles from them on the high rocky bank of a little stream. A hill of cedars rose behind his house. From his door in the east he could see the Waterless Mountain with its long straight skyline. In the summer time the sun rose right out of the middle of the mountain and shone into Hasteen Sani's doorway.

One afternoon when Younger Brother was driving the sheep past Hasteen Sani's hogan, he noticed signs of a ceremony. In front of the hogan a hole about four feet wide had been dug in the ground. It was two feet deep and filled with hot coals which a happy-looking woman was taking out and laying to one side.

Younger Brother stopped to watch. He had never seen this before. The woman lined the round hole with green corn leaves. Other women came out of the hogan carrying pots of corn meal batter. It was all poured into the hole and covered

37

with more green leaves, after which the hot coals were put back.

The women were all gay and happy. Someone said to Younger Brother:

"The cake will be a good one. We bake it for the young daughter of Hasteen Sani. She has been grinding the corn meal for three days. Tell your people to come tonight."

The boy wondered what it was all about. He would ask Mother when he reached home. She would know what they were doing. She did know, of course, and she said with a good deal of interest:

"So the young daughter of Hasteen Sani is to have the sweet corn cake baked for her. We shall go to hear the songs."

After supper everyone prepared for the sing. Mother wore her purple plush jacket with all the silver buttons. She took time to brush Father's long hair for him and tied it with a new string. Then Elder Brother's hair was brushed and tied. He was looking finer than ever. He had a new silk handkerchief to tie around his hair.

Father hitched the horses to the wagon while Mother wrapped the baby on her cradle board. They had only two miles to go and arrived at Hasteen Sani's house just as the full moon rose from behind the Waterless Mountain.

Inside the hogan all the friends were sitting around the fire. Uncle was the medicine man and he had many young men singers with him. Some would sing for a while then rest and smoke tobacco which they rolled in corn husks. Then another group would take their place. This was to keep up all night.

No one must get sleepy because it was the rule to stay awake. Only those who kept awake all night could eat the corn cake in the morning.

Younger Brother had no trouble at first because he was so interested in everything. There was a lot to look at and a lot to hear. He liked the young daughter of Hasteen Sani. She was slim and tall. Her skin was brown and smooth like the acorn. Her hair was like the night sky. Her slender moccasined feet peeped out from her full skirt and her long fingers were covered with silver and turquoise rings.

It was her eyes that were the loveliest. They did not seem to see people but looked into space while the young men sang the sacred songs. Sometimes the fire looked at itself in her eyes and then the dark brown color changed into flame and made Younger Brother think of the eyes of the night that sometimes peered from dark places under the trees. He knew she could see things that were holy — the things the young men were singing about.

Elder Brother also thought she was beautiful, but he noticed how well her red velveteen jacket fitted her, following the curves of her young body. He liked her eyes best when they looked at him, with half-lowered lids fringed with a curtain of darkness. He was glad he had worn the new red handkerchief on his head.

Just before day everyone except the girl went outside. The singers sang of the dawn and the Turquoise Woman and everybody was happy. At the end of the second song, the young daughter of Hasteen Sani held back the blanket that curtained the doorway and ran as fast as her little feet would carry her. She ran east toward the dawn.

Several young men raced with her. Elder Brother was the only one who caught up with her as she ran to the dawn. Then they all came back just as the sun sent its first rays over the Waterless Mountain to shine in Hasteen Sani's open door.

Younger Brother was watching everything. He saw the woman who had baked the cake remove the coals. He smelled the sweet steam rising from the ground. So did two little fuzzy dogs who ran too close to the cake hoping to have some also. The woman frightened them away with a corn-cob lying near. She threw it at them and they ran away yelping. Everyone laughed. Everyone was gay and happy.

The corn leaves were lifted from the top of the cake and there it was all brown and hot and four feet across. Younger Brother thought he could not wait for his share but he had to wait until the baker woman cut a circular piece right out of the center. She cut that in four pieces, gave one to Uncle because he was the medicine man, one to the girl because it was her cake, and the other two pieces to her father and mother.

Younger Brother watched the young girl. He thought she was more beautiful than ever with the sun touching her acorn brown cheeks. Elder Brother was standing near and he was very much surprised and very shy when the girl took her corn cake and gave it to him.

Everyone laughed except the two brothers and the girl. To them a very serious thing was happening. The girl was hoping that Elder Brother's father would send a present to her father.

She ran east toward the dawn.

The young man was bewildered. He did not understand. Younger Brother, looking at them, was reminded of the deer that danced in the sunlight. He didn't know why he thought of the deer; maybe it was because the two young people looked as if they would like to leap and run away as the deer had done.

While he was thinking, the baker woman handed him a piece of the corn cake. Everyone had a piece and people were getting ready to go home. Younger Brother was so sleepy he hoped someone would help herd the sheep. He even fell asleep in the wagon as Father drove home.

After that day there was much talk between Father and Mother and Uncle. It was time for Elder Brother to marry and Father must decide whom he should marry. She must be of an industrious, clean family and belong to a clan outside of theirs.

They thought Hasteen Sani's daughter would be a very good wife for their son. So it was decided that Father should talk to Hasteen Sani about it, which he did. Everything was settled and the present suggested was acceptable. Father was to give ten fine ponies to Hasteen Sani.

Younger Brother looked forward to the wedding. He wondered what it would be like. Mother had told him that Elder Brother would not live at home after the wedding. He would have a hogan of his own and the girl would live in it. It would be her hogan too and she would have her own sheep to look after.

Younger Brother thought that would be very nice and he asked Mother if he too could live there sometimes. She laughed and said he must live in Mother's hogan until he was a man like Elder Brother. He knew that Mother was always right about everything so thought no more about it.

He only wished that the beautiful young daughter of Hasteen Sani lived where he lived, because he had seen the far-away look in her eyes when she ran toward the dawn. He was sure she could understand the treasures hidden deep in the cave and he knew she could dance with the Star Children or the Deer People, or mount the sun rays that led to the home of Yellow Beak.

For the first time in his life Younger Brother felt lonely. He wanted to share his treasure cave with someone who understood. Quietly he walked to the cliff and climbed on the big boulders. He crawled in the small opening and sat down on the floor of the cave.

He took the little cloud bowl from the ledge. He had added two more treasures to his collection. The ruby-red stone was there and beside it lay a pure white arrow head which he had found on the mesa, but most precious of all was a little silver button that had fallen from the girl's moccasin when she raced to the dawn.

CHAPTER VIII

THE TRAIL OF BEAUTY

VER SINCE Younger Brother had made a new song, he was aware of many wonders in the world. Uncle had named him Little Singer, but that was a secret between them. That was a sacred name and not until he was a grown man, wise enough to be a medicine man, could he be called Little Singer by anyone but Uncle, his teacher. Singing was very important. He knew that, and since he had made a song himself he noticed that everything in the world sang.

As he sat in his little treasure cave holding the cloud bowl in his hands, he could hear a canyon wren trilling his sweet sad song. He could hear a locust chirruping in the sunshine. If things did not sing they danced to the silent music that filled all the air. He could tell by the way animals walked that they were keeping time to some kind of music. Maybe it was the song in their own hearts that they walked to.

The music in the poplar tree when the wind blew made all the little leaves dance merrily. To be alive meant to sing and

43

dance.   Uncle had told him that and had let him put his head to Uncle's heart to feel it dancing.

He remembered how wildly his own heart had danced when he saw the deer leaping in the sunshine, and he remembered how his new song was born at the sight.   Singing was good. It made one brother to the wind, the locusts, the birds, and the coyote.

Coyote was a mighty singer.   He could make the clouds weep.   He was hard to understand because he had done so many tricky things.   Many people disliked him.   He had been badly treated by his enemies but he was always ready for a new adventure, and he could always sing with his nose pointed upward.

Most all people looked upward when they sang.   Singers were like growing things on top of the earth.   They reached upward to the sun.   Everything that was alive and healthy reached upward and sang.

Younger Brother always liked to watch the coyote when he lifted his nose to the skies and made the clouds weep, and he liked to hear Uncle tell the story of the Young Woman Who Tinkles.

She was the wife of the original coyote whom the Navahos call Mai.   She wore a fine white buckskin dress with a fringe of deer hoofs on the skirt.   When she walked or ran, the deer hoofs tinkled and rattled like sweet music.   That is why Mai called her the Young Woman Who Tinkles.   He was very proud of his young wife, and he came to think the music of her presence the sweetest music in all the world.

One day Mai was alone in a forest of spruce and pine trees, high in the mountains. Many birds were chattering in the trees and playing a game that Mai had never seen before. They would pull out their eyes, throw them to the top of the trees and then call, "Drop back, my eyes ! Drop back !" The eyes would drop back right where they belonged.

Mai thought that was a wonderful game. He wanted to play it and asked the birds to pull out his eyes. They didn't want to play the game with him but he begged so hard they finally consented. Four times they took out his eyes and threw them up. When he called to them, "Drop back, my eyes ! Drop back!" they fell right into place again and he could see as well as ever.

Mai thought what a fine game that would be to show to his wife so he asked the birds to take his eyes out again. They were bothered by him and angry so the fifth time they took out his eyes they pulled the strings with them and tied them together.

When the eyes were thrown to the top of the tree the string caught on a branch and the eyes staid there. Poor Mai cried in vain, "Drop back, my eyes ! Drop back !" They never dropped back and he sat there howling, with his nose pointed upward.

Finally the cruel birds took pity on him and rolled some hard pine gum into two balls just the size of the coyote's eyes. These they stuck into the empty sockets. They were not very good eyes but Mai could see well enough to start for home. The gum was yellow and that is why coyotes have yellow eyes today.

On the way home Mai stopped at the home of his brother-in-law. He was cooking meat and offered some to Mai to roast. Mai leaned too near the fire and his pine gum eyes melted. His brother-in-law saw what had happened but he was not sorry because he did not like Mai. He had not wanted his sister to marry him. He thought, "Here is a chance to get rid of the troublesome fellow."

He led the blind Mai toward his home. When he reached there he took his sister's tinkling dress and gave it to a chicken hawk to carry in his beak. The chicken hawk rattled the dress in front of Mai. He thought his dear wife was there and he ran to greet her, but the chicken hawk kept out of reach, rattling the dress until he came to the edge of a deep canyon. Then he flew right over and poor blind Mai, following the rattling noise, stepped off the precipice and fell to the bottom of the canyon. He fell, calling the name of his beautiful Young Woman Who Tinkles.

Younger Brother always felt sorry for Coyote and he liked to think of the beautiful young woman. He wondered if she were as lovely as the young daughter of Hasteen Sani whom Elder Brother was soon to marry. It must be very soon because Mother had been making new clothes for all the family.

Just then, looking from the cave, he noticed a cloud of dust rising in the wash. Someone was driving horses. The dust moved nearer and nearer and from his secret place high above the floor of the valley, Younger Brother could recognize Father.

He had been out all day rounding up his ponies. They went running past the rocks to the corral with their heads held high

and their manes flying in the wind. Father looked very proud
and straight in the saddle. Not many men could give ten fine
ponies for a wedding present and still have enough left to make
him wealthy.

Younger Brother knew that if the ponies were left in the
corral it must be nearly time for the wedding. He put his
treasures all in place and climbed down from the cliff. At
home he found everyone busy. Uncle was there. That was
good. Uncle said:

"Have you brought the root of the yucca?"

"Yes, Uncle. I dug it myself. It was growing near the hole
of the prairie dog."

"Good, my child. The water is ready. We can wash our
hair."

A fine lather was made from the root and Mother washed
everyone's hair. Then she brushed all the hair with the stiff
brush made of grass stems tightly bunched and tied. Uncle
gave Younger Brother a beautiful new velveteen shirt, whispering to him:

"It is right that Little Singer should be well dressed at his
brother's wedding."

"Do we soon go to Hasteen Sani's hogan?"

"Yes, my child, we start when the sun is two fingers above
the western horizon."

Mother drove the horses hitched to the wagon, for Father
must drive the ten ponies. They were a splendid sight, all of
them riding to the home of Hasteen Sani. Father rode first
on his best black horse whose bridle was mounted in turquoise

and silver. He was proudly driving the ten prancing ponies. Behind him came Mother and Baby and Younger Brother in the new red wagon bought at the trading post. It had the Big Man's name painted on it in black. Behind the wagon Uncle and Elder Brother rode on their ponies. Two of the sheep dogs trotted behind.

They traveled westward with the Sun on his way to the Turquoise Woman. Soon Elder Brother would be with his own woman who had raced him to the dawn. His heart sang the song of the Sun.

> *I travel a trail of beautiful thoughts.*
> *I walk to the ends of earth to your hearth.*
> *O woman of turquoise waiting for me*
> *I travel a trail of beautiful thoughts.*

CHAPTER IX

THE BASKET CEREMONY

OR DAYS the young daughter of Hasteen Sani had watched her mother preparing for the wedding. She had made new clothes for all the family, sewing bright-colored calico skirts for the women. Ten yards of cloth went into every skirt, with its ruffle reaching to the ground in brilliant splendor of orange bands.

The girl's skirt was lovely. It was the color of the garnets on the ant hills and trimmed with a finger-wide band of deep blue. Her jacket of apple-green plush made a perfect background for the heavy turquoise necklace that her mother had given her.

The mother was so busy she had little time to think about losing her daughter. She wished she could be at the wedding but Navaho custom does not permit the mother-in-law of the husband ever to be in his presence. She must never be seen by him. When he is away she may visit her daughter, but only when he is away. So she must be content doing things for the girl.

Two new log hogans had been built, one for the ceremony and one for the bride to live in.

Mutton was stewing in pots and ready to roast over the fire. Blue cornmeal dumplings were rolled and ready to boil and sweet green corn was to be roasted in the coals. Stewed dried peaches scented the air. Watermelons and muskmelons were piled against the log wall. There was plenty to eat, for every guest must have his fill and be able to take something home in a flour sack.

As darkness crept over the Waterless Mountain, the family, waiting outside the hogan, could hear the horses and the wagon coming down the road, which wound its way among stunted cedars.

Soon, on top of a rocky knoll, the first of the prancing ponies ran into the light of the campfire. Then the rest appeared, with Father on his black horse skillfully driving them to Hasteen Sani's corral. The firelight gleamed on his silver bridle. Everyone thought what a fine marriage this is.

Wealth was to be added to wealth, beauty to beauty.

The girl's mother hid behind the hogan where she could not be seen by her son-in-law, but she couldn't help peeking out to look at the ten beautiful ponies.

Then came all the rest of the party.

When everything was ready for the ceremony, Elder Brother lifted the blanket hanging over the entrance to the new hogan. He lifted it on the north side, entered the sweet cedar log house with its fire in the center, walked from the east to the south and sat on a blanket spread west of the fire.

The first of the prancing ponies ran into the light of the campfire.

While he sat there, still singing in his heart the song of the
Sun Bearer, the bride entered with her father.   She walked on
the south side of the fire and sat on the blanket beside Elder
Brother.

Then all the friends and relatives came in and sat all around.
It was a big party.

When everyone was seated, Hasteen Sani placed a shallow
basket of cornmeal porridge in front of the young couple.   On
this porridge he drew a line of white corn pollen from east to
west and back again.   Then he crossed the white line with
yellow corn pollen from south to north and back again.

Next he drew a circle with yellow pollen around the cross,
beginning in the east and going to south and west and north
and completing it in the east.   Because the sun travels that way,
it is the right way.

After Hasteen Sani had drawn the cross and circle on the
basket of porridge, he placed an old pottery jar of water and a
gourd ladle in front of his daughter.   She dipped the water
with the ladle and poured it over Elder Brother's hands while
he washed them.   Then he did the same for her.

After that Hasteen Sani turned the east side of the wedding
basket toward the couple and Elder Brother took a pinch of the
porridge from the east end of the line of pollen.   He ate it and
then his bride did the same thing.

After that they tasted from the south, west and north.   Elder
Brother's hand was followed by the girl's in its journey around
the circle of life.

The ceremony was finished.   The wedding was over.   Elder

Brother and the beautiful young daughter of Hasteen Sani were husband and wife. She looked very shy and lovelier than ever.

During all this time, Younger Brother watched everything, as he always did. He was proud of his handsome brother and his beautiful new sister. He did not know whether the far-away look was in her eyes because she kept them cast down.

After all the relatives had finished talking and advising the young couple and everyone sat about eating and having a jolly time, Younger Brother slipped up to the girl. While no one was looking he gave her a present.

It was a most precious deer hoof he had found under the brush on the Waterless Mountain. He told the daughter of Hasteen Sani that the Young Woman Who Tinkles had sent it to her for a wedding present, and of course she believed him. She tied it on the fringe of her red woven belt and looked up at Younger Brother with the far-away look in her eyes.

He knew she could understand.

CHAPTER X

THE PACK RAT

IT WAS certainly lonely at the hogan by the juniper tree. Younger Brother missed the big brother who had always sat in a special place by the fire, telling of his hunting and riding adventures. Mother was the loneliest of all. It seemed as if she could not endure the absence of her laughing brown-eyed son, who used to bring her such good game to cook.

But then everyone was talking about the wedding. They said it was the best basket ceremony for many a year. There was comfort in that.

The first frost had whitened the round dome of the hogan and silvered the rims of the wagon wheels. The voice of the thunder was still and the snakes no longer listened to the words of men. It was safe to tell the sacred stories again.

Every night Uncle came to teach Younger Brother the songs of the medicine men. The little boy liked to hear about Reared-within-the-Mountain. That is the name of a holy young man whose friends were the bears and all the other

mountain animals. They all helped Reared-within-the-Mountain to hide from his enemies the Utes.

Younger Brother liked the Pack Rat story.

The Pack Rat lived under a flat rock on the hillside. There
were little sticks and stones piled all around his nest. One day
the Pack Rat saw Reared-within-the-Mountain running toward
his house. He knew he was in trouble.

"Hide me quickly," said the boy.

The Pack Rat said, "Lie down by the hole to my house."

It was such a small hole the boy couldn't crawl in, so the
Pack Rat puffed out his cheeks and his chest and blew a long,
strong breath on the entrance to make it large enough for the
boy to enter.

Inside the house the Rat People were kind to him. They
offered him food, which he couldn't think of eating — chips
and bones and shells of seeds and skins of fruit. The boy
wouldn't eat any of them. He noticed a long row of wicker
jars standing on the floor.

"What is in that black jar at the end of the row ?" he asked.

The Rat Woman removed the top of the jar and took out
some splendid piñon nuts and fruit of the yucca.

"That is fine," said the boy. "What is in the white jar ?"

"Cherries and cactus fruit. Will you have some ?"

The boy was very hungry and was about to eat the cherries
and nuts and fruit when the wind whispered to him:

"Do not eat the food of the rat in the home of the rat or you
will turn into a rat."

So the boy, hungry as he was, put the nice food in a corner of his buckskin robe.

Just about that time his enemy thrust a long stick through the little hole of the rat's nest but nobody was hurt and the enemy became tired and went away before dark.

Younger Brother always liked the Pack Rat People after Uncle told him that story.

One day when he was climbing up the boulders that led to his cave, he saw a Pack Rat scampering from the cliff. He watched the rat to see in what direction he ran. After the boy was in the cave, he noticed little tracks of the rat in the soft dust that had settled on the floor. The tracks led right around the edge of the cave and stopped at the north where the piece of shiny black petrified wood should be. The little shiny black treasure was not there.

Younger Brother was frightened. He knew the Pack Rat had taken the treasure away. Then he remembered how kind the Pack Rats had been to Reared-within-the-Mountain. If he thought right about this it would be all right. Probably the rat needed the shiny black piece for his own home.

That night when Uncle came, Younger Brother told him what had happened. That meant that Uncle must be told the secret about the cave and the treasures. He was the first one to share the secret and he said:

"Surely the Pack Rat had a reason for taking the black shiny piece from the north. Tomorrow, my child, go again to the cave and see what is there."

He went and imagine his surprise to find in the north a pure white pebble where his black petrified wood had been.

When he told Uncle about it that night, the wise medicine man looked serious and said:

"The Pack Rat must know his medicine. Sometimes we put the white color in the north and move the black to the east."

Uncle was very serious about it. He knew that his pupil was a chosen medicine man. Everything pointed that way. The deer had danced for him, Yellow Beak had sent him a tail feather, and now the Pack Rat was telling him about the black and white, and the north and east. Uncle believed that his Little Singer might be one of the holy ones. So he was very serious.

Not long after this the boy became ill. No one knew what was wrong. He couldn't take the sheep out. Mother must do it, with everything else she had to do. Uncle stayed with Younger Brother and Sister.

Uncle was puzzled about the boy. He lay on his sheepskin and said nothing. He ate nothing. After a while his face and hands became hot. Every day he grew hotter, till the fever in his head made him say queer things. He raved about his treasures in the cave, his feather, his red stone, and he raved about the Pack Rat. He was afraid the rat would take his strawberry jam picture.

Most often he cried, "Hasteen Tso, Hasteen Tso."

He was calling for the Big Man. "Hasteen Tso, Hasteen Tso, Hasteen Tso."

Mother took out the sheep.

Uncle told Father to ride to the trading post for help. At the post the Big Man was very busy trying to do something for everyone. A party of tourists was asking questions about every little thing. One wanted to know if the Indians still scalped people.

"I have never seen it done," said the Big Man as he went on addressing envelopes on his typewriter.

When the Navaho father entered, the trader's face softened. He shook hands with the Indian. No word was spoken for several minutes, then the father said:

"For four days Younger Brother eats nothing. He has heat in the head. His sleep is torn from him."

The Big Man listened patiently. Nearly every day someone was ill. There should be nurses to look after such cases. The father continued:

"He eats nothing and he calls, 'Hasteen Tso, Hasteen Tso.' Grandfather, will you see him?"

The Big Man was so very busy and he must take care of all the tourists. The Navaho still pleaded:

"Grandfather, you can make him well. He calls, 'Hasteen Tso.'"

"I must go," said the trader, turning to the tourists. "These people need me."

He cleared his desk, locked his safe, put some oranges in his car and a bottle of castor oil in his pocket.

When he reached the camp of Younger Brother's family, Mother had returned with the sheep. She was sitting on the floor beside her little sick boy, holding his fevered hand in her cool one. Uncle too was there, singing one of the sacred songs of the Deer People and keeping time with a gourd rattle.

The boy was moaning and calling, "Hasteen Tso" as the Big Man entered the hogan. The trader was glad he had come. He told Mother how to fix the medicine while he peeled an orange for the little sufferer. He had entered the hogan so quietly that the child had not heard him and his eyes were closed. When the orange was peeled it filled the room with such a sweet pungent odor that Younger Brother opened his eyes. They rested on the Big Man and a faint smile played about his lips. He put his little hot hands out and eagerly said:

"I want you to know about the Pack Rat. Maybe he took the picture with the red mountains."

The Big Man did not know what Younger Brother was talking about, but he smiled and said:

"I shall see about it, Grandchild, but first I want you to take the medicine and the sweet yellow fruit."

After that was done the Big Man sat by the little boy until he went to sleep. Then he asked Uncle if he knew about the picture with the red mountains, or about the Pack Rat.

"I do not know about the picture, but the Pack Rat is teaching our grandchild."

Then Uncle told the Big Man about the cave and they both went to see it. Neither one could crawl in because each was too big, but they could look in and reach everything. When the Big Man found the strawberry jam label in the little cloud bowl, he understood what was troubling Younger Brother.

He put everything back in place and added to the treasures

of the pottery bowl, a very blue turquoise bead he had been carrying in his pocket for years.

Uncle made sure that the four colors were placed as the Pack Rat wanted them and then the two big men left the cave. The white man said:

"Let the child rest for a while and he will be all right."

"Yes," said Uncle, "the spell is removed and he is restored in beauty. The Pack Rat is wise in his teachings. He made the child call you to help him."

The Big Man laughed and said to himself, "So it was the Pack Rat that saved me from those tourists."

CHAPTER XI

CHRISTMAS AT THE TRADING POST

OTHER took care of the sheep for several days till her little boy was strong enough to go out again. The clear calm days of fall brought health to Younger Brother. Summer stood back to back with winter. The earth months were finished, having yielded the lambs, the wool, and the corn. Only the piñons, those sweet little nuts of the single-leaved pine, remained to be gathered.

By the time the month of Slender Wind came, Younger Brother was well and strong and able to go to the piñon forests to help fill the sacks for the trader. He went with Elder Brother and his bride. Mother and Father stayed home with Baby Sister and the sheep.

The piñon pickers traveled by wagon and horseback to the forests high in the mountains. They camped under the trees, enjoying the clear sky and the still sunshine of the month of Slender Wind.

The ground beneath the trees was strewn with smooth brown

nuts which had fallen from the pine cones. Younger Brother worked with interest, hoping that Mother would take him to the trading post when she went to sell the piñons.

He wanted to see the Big Man again and tell him he had found the turquoise bead in the little pottery bowl. Uncle had told him that Hasteen Tso had put it there. Now that he shared the secret of his cave with Uncle and the white medicine man, he did not feel so lonely. He still remembered how good the sweet yellow fruit smelled.

While he was thinking about all these things, he noticed two young Navahos coming down the mountain with their arms full of spruce boughs. They loaded their horses with the spruce and rode away. Younger Brother knew there was to be a sing at Two Rivers where the spruce would be needed for the costumes of the Yays. The Yays always wore deerskin masks with spruce collars, when they danced in the Night Chant. Younger Brother remembered how sacred the spruce was when he was initiated the year before. He was glad he knew where it grew, because some day, when he had a horse of his own, he could gather spruce boughs for Uncle.

All through the month of Slender Wind the sun shone brightly. The nights were bitter cold and the campfires were kept burning all night. In the distance the coyotes sang their songs to the clouds. Then came the month of Big Wind. Still there was day after day of sunshine and the people of the earth traveled on, gathering piñons further back in the mountain.

Younger Brother enjoyed himself immensely. It was fun to

pick up the nuts and sift the dirt from them through a wire screen the trader had sent: and when it was time to eat, his new sister always had the coffee boiling on the campfire. She made good bread in the Dutch oven and roasted the mutton over the coals on a wire door mat from the store. She was very happy with her handsome husband and they played and laughed together like two children.

Younger Brother noticed that she still wore the deer hoof on the fringe of her red belt. There were little shells tied to the fringe also. Women always wore shells. That was to make them remember the White Shell Woman of the east. She was the younger sister of the Turquoise Woman of the west and was related to the water.

When the two sisters were young girls, they were all alone on a mountain top. They were very, very lonely. The Turquoise Woman looked at her lovely young sister and said:

"It is so lonely here. We have no one to speak to but ourselves. We see nothing but the orb that rolls over us in the sky, and the silver waterfall below us. I wonder if they can be people."

"I think they are people, sister," said the White Shell Woman, "for sometimes I hear the waterfall calling me softly. I feel that I must go to the waterfall. Sister, I am going."

The Turquoise Woman watched her little sister as her slender shell-white feet sped from stone to stone. She watched her crescent body sway in the sunshine along the rainbow trail of glistening spray. For one shining moment the maiden stood in all her whiteness against the shadowed rocks. The Turquoise Woman waved goodby to her, for she knew that no more would they dance together on the mountain tops.

Her loneliness was more than she could bear and she threw herself on the hot rocks and cried to the sun, "Come to me, come."

After that the sisters were not lonely, for the waterfall gave the gentle Child of the Water to the White Shell Woman, and the sun gave the Turquoise Woman a most glorious shining young god of light. These two boys had always helped the Navahos and Younger Brother liked the stories of their adventures the best of all, and he liked their mothers, who were so kind and beautiful.

As he watched his brother's wife laughing in the sunshine with him, he thought she was like the Turquoise Woman, but when she looked at Younger Brother, he knew she was the White Shell Woman, who loved the water and cool, quiet places of mystery. That was why he knew she would understand his innermost thoughts about his treasures.

The piñons were nearly gathered and there came a bitter cold spell. The people suffered. One little baby had its feet frozen. The young mother rode horseback for two days till she reached the post. There the trader's sister rubbed oil on the little feet and cried a bit because she loved all the babies. She loved them so much she was making Christmas presents for them.

She told the young mother to let all the other mothers know there would be a Christmas tree and gifts for all the children in seven days.

The Navahos counted how many times the sun set, and bright and early on Christmas morning, they began to arrive at the post.

Fathers drove their wagons from miles around and many little children were in every wagon. The piñon pickers were through for the year and they came with hundreds of pounds of nuts in sacks.

Younger Brother was there with Mother and Baby Sister. No one knew what Christmas meant. It was a day when white people seemed kinder and did not ask for money when they gave the children apples and candy.

Inside the store a fire was burning in the big stove and coffee was boiling for everyone. The place was crowded with children and someone was telling them that soon the door would be opened and they could see the tree. They could hear people laughing and talking in the other room. They wondered what the tree was. They were such wild little children they felt uncomfortable, even afraid. They liked trees out of doors but wondered what kind of tree grew inside a room.

Then the door opened and there stood a dark green tree all blooming with little fires. On the very top a great star glittered. It was really enough to frighten any child of the woods who had never before seen a tree of fire, but when a terrible-looking fat Yay jumped right in front of the tree and jingled little bells, all the children began to cry.

Younger Brother was braver than the rest and he looked at everything. He noticed that the Yay had on a red mask with white hair and whiskers. His clothes were bright red trimmed with white fur. He was taking little bags of candy and nuts off the tree. Such queer things grew on that tree that it was a long time before Younger Brother recognized it as a spruce.

When he did, he remembered the spruce boughs gathered on the mountain. He remembered how the stars shone through the trees at night and how a big star once rested on the very top of a dark tree. Then he began to feel at home. This must be the white man's way of using the sacred spruce for a ceremonial.

Navaho Yays were kindly. Probably this white Yay, whom they called Santa Claus, was all right. Thinking this way, Younger Brother became brave enough to accept a bag of candy. Then the other little children followed his example and soon everyone was eating candy and apples, and blowing tin horns or chewing the ends of them. There were pink celluloid rattles for the babies, tin buckets and shovels and a little tin man that could walk.

The white lady at the post was very happy watching the children and had almost forgotten how lonely she was for her own little girl away at school in the city. Suddenly she remembered and before she knew what was happening, a big tear rolled down her cheek. An old Navaho man noticed that she was crying and said to her:

"Little Sister, you cry because your child is away. We know what that means. When our children go away to school, the mothers cry also."

The white lady listened in wonder as the old man turned to his people in the store and spoke to them.

"My grandchildren, our white sister is sad. She cries for

her child. We will all give money to have her child brought back."

Every Navaho gave something and the old man handed the collection to the white lady. This made her cry more than ever, but when she saw that the kindly people of the earth were mystified by her tears, she smiled and called the Big Man from his office to tell them how happy she was at their thought.

Younger Brother watched the Big Man and waited for the smile. It came like a shaft of sunlight on the mountain. He thanked the Navahos for their kindness to his sister and then he turned to her. She said:

"Didn't I always say the spirit of Christmas would win even a savage ?"

The Big Man put his arm around his little sister, smiled and answered:

"Didn't I always say that these people traveled the trail of beauty ?"

Younger Brother still watched the Big Man's face and deep in his heart he knew that all medicine men are beautiful, white or brown, and he knew that spruce trees meant health and happiness to everyone who understands. He remembered hearing his uncle sing this song from the Mountain Chant:

> *He brings a treasure to me,*
> *The holy one brings to me*
> *A dark spruce sapling,*
> *A treasure he brings to me.*

CHAPTER XII

THE GIANT DRAGON FLY

HREE winters had stood back to back with three summers, since Younger Brother had first gathered piñons in the mountains. He had reached the age of twelve years and he rode his own pony when he herded the sheep. Riding the pony was a big help to the shepherd because it gave him companionship. He and the pony became acquainted. Just herding sheep day by day, month by month, and year by year can become very tiresome, but Younger Brother managed all right because he had his songs to practice. They must be perfect. There were hundreds of words to memorize and some of the words had no meaning. He must learn them by sound.

So sometimes when he was away on the mesas with the sheep, he would be singing at the top of his voice:

Hoo nen no ho nen
no ha,
Hoo nen no ho nen
no na.

The sounds meant nothing in human speech, but they must have meant a great deal to the birds for they always stopped to listen. Younger Brother noticed this and it made him think. If he could talk animal language he would be able to learn secrets that no one knew. Most of all he wanted to know the secret of flying, so he set about to watch the birds both great and small.

One summer day after he had taken the sheep home for Mother to look after, he walked up a narrow canyon where he had noticed signs of moisture under the rocks. He wanted to trace the water to its source. He climbed over rocks and up cliffs where no one had ever been before. He was hot and tired but he kept climbing because he was seeking the source of the water.

He had just managed to pull himself up an extra steep place by hanging on to a ledge with his hands, when he saw what he was seeking. He found the pool. It was nearly at the top of the cliffs which culminated in a flat level floor.

The pool was deep and dark and there was no telling what strange shapes might be lurking beneath its surface. There could be anything in that pool, from little yellow water snakes to dark slimy monsters that never saw the light. It seemed to be a bottomless pit.

The water was clear and pure, flowing just enough to nourish tender green things in its neighborhood. Delicate maidenhair ferns grew under the limestone ledge back of the pool and the softest musk-scented plants bloomed where the sun touched a

little bit.   The flowers were pale yellow velvety mimulus, radi-
ating a golden light among the shadowed rocks.

These fairy-like plants were not trampled upon, for the rocky
canyon was so inaccessible that no cattle could reach it for
feeding.   Such pools are always beyond the reach of cattle.
Only creatures of the air know of their existence.   Only
winged creatures who can look down from above know the
beauty of deep hidden pools.

Younger Brother was hot and tired.   His body was bruised
and his feet were cut a little by the sharp stones, but he was
happy because he had found the pool.   He sat down to rest.
He leaned his head back against the trunk of an oak tree and
drowsily looked at the sky showing in turquoise spots through
the green leaves of the oak.

He sat there some time, feeling drowsier and drowsier.   He
was very still, just resting and thinking how fortunate were the
birds who could fly to a place like this.   Just then a red-tailed
wood-pecker flew down to the water to drink.   His tail was
like red sun rays shining out of a dark cloud.   He was a splendid young chief.

Younger Brother whistled very softly to the bird.   The wood-
pecker put his head on one side, listening, and then hopped
right up on the boy's knee.

"How do you fly, brother ?   I want to know."

The wood-pecker spread his wings and flew to the top of the
tree.   Younger Brother watched him, sadly saying, "It is so
easy for you."

Pretty soon he heard a chattering in the tree above him.   All the little birds were screaming at a big yellow-tailed hawk that was gliding through the air. The boy carefully watched him. He was not even moving his wings.

"Oh, how do you fly, heaven-born ?" the boy asked as the hawk swooped down to the tree.

No one could answer him. Always there were questions, questions, which no one could answer.

Uncle had once said, "There are flying things and crawling things and swimming things and walking things. Each should be strong in his own way. Of the walking things, man is the weakest because his feet are tied to the ground and his thoughts fly to the clouds."

Younger Brother knew the wisdom of Uncle and his teachings, but no one answered the questions that filled his mind. Why couldn't he fly in the daytime when he was awake? He could fly so beautifully at night in his dreams.

The only answer was that he was earth-born and he wished he were sky-born. But he had never given up hope that he might some day be lifted off the earth to float around with the clouds.

He was feeling very drowsy and he must have fallen asleep for a minute. He didn't remember just what happened for a little while, but he was aroused by a sound something like distant thunder. The noise grew louder and louder.

Younger Brother was puzzled. A shadow was passing over the still pool. A wing-like form was moving across its surface and the burring, buzzing noise filled the air and echoed among the rocks.

The boy looked up in terror and saw such a monstrous, winged creature, he thought it must be Tse na ha le, the harpy of the old stories. He hid his face in his arms. He crouched by the oak tree not daring to stir nor look up. In a few minutes everything was quiet for a while. Then he heard a voice in the air above. It was a man's voice speaking the words of white men.

Younger Brother could not understand the words, but he recognized the voice. He knew the Big Man was talking. He was saying:

"This mesa top makes an excellent landing field and I know there must be water near. Those tree tops suggest it."

"Suppose we climb down and see," said a second voice.

Younger Brother sat perfectly still. He was not frightened now that the Big Man was near. He could hear the two men scrambling down the rocks. When they reached the pool Younger Brother stood up. He certainly startled the men.

"How on earth did you get here ? Did you fly, Grandchild ?"

"No, Grandfather. I climbed up from the valley on my hands and feet."

"Why did you come, child ?"

"To find the water."

The Big Man looked at the pool and said to the government water developer who was with him:

"It's a better supply than I dreamed of, Conklin. It would water a thousand head of sheep a day. I wonder if it could be piped to the valley below."

Turning to Younger Brother he asked, "Is the trail very steep ?"

"Very steep and narrow and the rocks cut my moccasins."

"How are you going to get down, child ?   Looks as if you would need wings for that."

"I have no wings, Grandfather."

"But I have and I will loan them to you."

He turned to the water developer and asked, "Is there room in the plane for the little fellow ?"

"Guess we can make it but you'll have to hold him in."

"Come along then, child.   We will find the big bird."

Younger Brother thought he must still be dreaming but he did as he was told, climbing up to the top of the cliffs with the men.   When they were on top he saw the great wings of the plane about half a mile away.

They shone like the wings of Tanilai the dragon fly. Younger Brother knew he was dreaming.   He walked close to the Big Man.   When they reached the dragon fly, they both climbed into the body of the fly and the strange man climbed in back of them.   The fly began to buzz, louder and louder.

Younger Brother grasped the Big Man's sleeve and hid his head on his friend's shoulder.

"Look, look, Grandchild, we fly."

He looked and there were mesas, mountains and trees running away.   Everything was running away except a big fluffy white cloud in the east.   That stood still and the dragon fly buzzed nearer and nearer to it.   Then before Younger Brother knew what was happening, they were on the cloud.

Then he realized that his wish had been granted.   His feet
were off the earth and his head was in the clouds.   He was so
excited and happy he sang the song of the Holy Young Man
who sought the Gods and found them.   On the summits of the
clouds he sought the Gods and found them.

The Big Man was just as happy as the little boy and he sang
the song with him.

> *On the summits of the clouds*
> *He sought the gods and found them.*
> *With a prayer within his heart*
> *He sought the gods and found them.*
> *Somebody doubts it so I have heard.*

"We do not doubt it, do we, Grandchild ?" said the Big Man
as he put his arm around the little Navaho boy whose wishes
always came true.

There are always doubters but what of it, so long as there
are those who believe and dream?   Younger Brother had flown
to the summits of the clouds with the Big Man.   They had
sung together.

More than that, the boy had scattered pollen on the clouds
and prayed, "You who dwell in the house of dark cloud, I am
your child.   Be kind to my people and be kind to Hasteen Tso,
too."

CHAPTER XIII

WATER FROM THE POOL

S THE giant dragon fly floated down to earth, Younger Brother waved goodby to the clouds. The Big Man drove him home in his car. Mother was happy to see them for she had been wondering what had become of her little son. When he told her that a giant dragon fly had carried him to the clouds, she laughed. Of course she didn't believe him. She said to the Big Man:

"The child is crazy. Always he is dreaming."

"No, Mother, he is not crazy. What the child says is true for I was with him. We flew in a white man's machine."

Father had been listening. He said:

"It is true, for when I rode after the horses today, I saw the dragon fly as it buzzed into the clouds. Now I know that white men are mightier than Navahos. We can ride and shoot and work with silver, but we cannot fly."

When Uncle came, Younger Brother told him of his adventure. Privately he spoke of sprinkling pollen on the clouds.

74

"That was right, child. Tell me, were there paintings on the clouds ?"

"Yes, there was color in the east, south, west and north, but the pattern was not clear for the clouds were not all unrolled."

Uncle was much impressed. His pupil was teaching him. Had not the Holy Ones painted on clouds ?

The Four Children of the Sky had made the first paintings on clouds. The Navahos could not paint on clouds. They must use the earth and earth colors. They must paint with colored sands on the floor of the medicine lodge but the Sons of the Sky had taught the designs and colors to the early people of the earth.

Uncle was teaching his Little Singer how to pour the sand from between his thumb and forefinger. Every Navaho boy learns to paint with sand.

After that day of flying Younger Brother's head was full of so many things that his sheep would have suffered had he not cared for them unconsciously. So many years of herding had made it second nature to the boy. Besides the flying to the clouds, he had the pool to think about. He wondered if it went deep, deep down to the underworld where the race of the ancients lived.

He believed it held secrets that would make people happy. The Big Man knew that it did. He knew there was life in that pool to nourish many if the water could be piped to the valley. The water developer also believed it and decided to do what seemed impossible. Day after day he loaded his plane with pipes and tools and cement, and flew to the mesa top to work.

He was a civil engineer and a good climber. He found the best way to get the water down and made a cement reservoir in the valley under the rocks near Younger Brother's cave. This did not trouble the boy so much as it would have when he was smaller, as he had grown too big to crawl into his cave and had removed his treasures to Uncle's hogan where they were kept with Uncle's medicine bundles.

When the reservoir was finished and filled with water, every-one felt like having a celebration, so it was decided to hold the Anadji, or war dance there. In olden times the Anadji was held for wounded warriors, but now it is given for weakness and swooning.

Hasteen Sani was in need of the ceremony, for he had looked on the slain body of his pony. High in the mountains the Soft-footed Chief had killed the pony and Hasteen Sani was very much shocked. He felt sure that the sing would restore him.

Everyone kept busy getting ready. Father made a new silver buckle to wear on his belt. Cedar boughs were hauled for building the cooking shelter for the women. Uncle was to be the medicine man. He told Younger Brother about the origin of the ceremony, which celebrates the combat between the sons of the Turquoise Woman and Yaytso the big giant.

Yaytso was destroying all the people of the earth, so the Sun Bearer gave weapons of lightning to his two boys and they started out to clear the world of trouble. First they went to the mountain of the south where the terrible Yaytso lived.

They hid in a cave waiting for the giant to go for his daily drink in the valley.

He was so big that when he leaned down to drink he rested one hand on top of the southern mountain and the other on some hills across the valley. His feet stretched away as far as a man could walk between sunrise and noon.

The two boys were sure they could conquer this giant because they had faith in the weapons their father had given them. They had shot one of the lightning arrows at the southern mountain, and it had made a great cleft in the side that is there to this day.

They watched the giant drink. Every time he stooped with his mouth to the water, the lake grew smaller. Four times he drank and the lake was nearly drained. So amazed were the boys to see how much water Yaytso drank that they lost their presence of mind and failed to shoot while he was stooping over the water. They went to the edge of the lake as he took his last swallow and he saw their reflections in the water.

The giant raised his head and roared, "What a pretty pair have come in sight ! Where have I been hunting that I never saw them before ? Yin-i-ke-to-ko — fee-fo-fum — yin-i-ke-to-ko — fee-fo-fum."

The boys listened and called back, "What a great thing has come in sight ! Where have we been hunting ?"

Four times the giant taunted the boys, and four times they answered back. They were having a great time, standing on an arched rainbow. Just then they heard the wind whispering, "Beware, beware." Just in time they flattened the rainbow out till it touched the ground, for Yaytso had hurled a lightning bolt that passed clear over their heads.

Up and down bounced the rainbow with the boys on top, and every time the giant hurled a bolt it missed the boys, either going above the rainbow or under it.

It was a lively combat. The boys succeeded in sending a chain-lightning arrow at the giant, who tottered toward the east. A second arrow made him stumble toward the south. He recovered his balance and was about to hurl another bolt himself, when the boys sent a shaft into him causing him to fall on his knees in the west. The fourth arrow was the last, and Yaytso lay on his face in the north, moving no more.

The boys had slain the first monster. Scattered bits of flint lay all around him for his flint armor had been shivered into pieces. After the two mighty Children of the Sun had scalped the giant, they put his broken arrows in a basket with his scalp and started for home.

When they arrived they hung the basket on a tree and went to meet their mother, the Turquoise Woman. They were about to tell her what they had done when they both fell in a faint. The mother knew how to bring them back to consciousness. She made medicine of plants that had been struck by lightning. This she sprinkled over the boys and shot a spruce arrow over their bodies. Then she shot a pine arrow over them and they were well.

Younger Brother was glad Uncle told him the story of the Children of the Sun. He liked to understand why his people held their ceremonies. Now he knew that the Anadji is given for anyone who has swooned or grown weak at the sight of violence.

Uncle let him help trim the juniper stick which was to be carried in the dance of the maidens.

CHAPTER XIV

THE DANCE OF THE MAIDENS

HE FULL moon rose from behind a hill of cedars and spread a silver blanket over the desert. In the center of the silver blanket a red cross of fire radiated its light to an encircling mass of Navahos, with their horses and wagons behind them. The full moon heard the songs of the young men who stood in two groups facing each other. Arm in arm and close together they swayed to the rhythm of their songs, while the leader beat on an old pottery drum.

The full moon saw a little Navaho maiden enter the firelight, carrying a juniper wand which Younger Brother had helped to make. It was trimmed with turkey feathers and sagebrush and long streamers of red cotton cloth.

The little maid was very serious and dignified. She held her head high. Her moccasined feet moved slowly across the sand until she approached the singers. She waved her wand and a young girl from the crowd of onlookers moved toward the men and chose one for her partner in the dance. Other girls followed her example.

The men were shy. They hung their heads in shame. They were reluctant to dance but the girls pulled them into the firelight and the quiet sober dance began while the little wand bearer kept time with her wand.

The full moon looked down on the maidens as they danced, and on the mothers sitting by, wrapped in their gayly-colored shawls. As the silver orb rolled westward through the night, the young men sang and sang till dawn.

Everyone was sleepy in the gray morning but the mothers were cooking in the green cedar shelters. Coffee was hot and bread was ready. At little campfires outside the shelter, families ate their breakfast and talked of the dance of the girls.

Younger Brother having helped in the ceremony before the dance could eat no meat, nor salt, nor sugar, nor hot things. He could have only corn and cold water for four days after the ceremony.

He was thinking how beautiful the wand had looked swaying in the firelight, and he was only half-conscious of the beauty of the girl who carried it. She had seemed so much a part of its grace that he did not separate them in his thoughts. She had held the wand high and had not once let it touch the ground. After the dance she had ridden toward the north on her pony, still holding the wand in her hand.

For three nights the girls danced but in different places. Hasteen Sani, the patient, stayed in the medicine lodge to be treated by Uncle. Of course he grew better and everyone was happy at the new water tank.

Sheep drank from the overflow, horses from the trough, and

the people carried buckets of water from the covered tank to their camps.

Four days after the ceremony was over, Elder Brother and his wife and their two-year-old baby came to spend the day with Mother. Little Sister loved the baby. It was good to have someone besides her lamb to play with. Every spring Mother had given her a lamb for a playmate. In time she would own a flock of her own. Already she was learning to herd them.

She played with her lamb as a white child plays with a doll, only it was much better, because the lamb could run and jump into the air on its funny stiff legs. It could drink milk from a bottle and get into all kinds of mischief.

While Sister played with Elder Brother's baby, the lamb was chewing the cork in a vinegar bottle. Mother had bought the vinegar to put in her dye.

The cork must have been just what the lamb wanted, for he gave it such a hard bite the bottle fell over and all the vinegar ran out on the floor.

He thought it was water, but when he tasted it he jumped right up in the air and bleated, "Ma, Ma." He ran outside with Sister chasing him. She was laughing and looking very pretty with her black hair blowing in the wind and her bare brown feet skipping in and out from under her long full skirt.

She caught the lamb on top of a little hill and sat down all out of breath, holding him tightly in her arms. When Younger Brother came with the sheep, the lamb jumped away to run to its mother in the flock. Sister went into the hogan to play with the baby.

The whole family was home and they sat around the fire drinking coffee and talking of the wonder of the new water, the success of the girls' dance, and of Younger Brother's flight to the clouds.

Uncle said, "My Little Singer brought the water to us, because he sprinkled pollen on the clouds and prayed for the good of all of us."

No one would think of disputing the wise medicine man, but Father couldn't help saying:

"But he flew in the white man's machine. We Navahos cannot fly."

Uncle answered, "We can sprinkle pollen and pray. Each has his power. Little Singer is the first Navaho to fly to the clouds and the first to sprinkle pollen on them."

"That is true," said Father.

Mother was worried. If her child traveled on clouds, he must be one of the Holy People. They traveled on rainbows and sunbeams, and they always left the earth to the people of the earth.

She wanted to keep her child. She showed him the new saddle blanket she had woven for his pony. It was gray with black and white cloud patterns twisting across its surface. Mother told her boy they were summer clouds on a summer sky. She said the red squares in the corners were sunlight.

"Put it on your pony and be satisfied to ride on the earth,

my son. See, I have made red sunbeam tassels to hang from the corners."

"It is a good weaving, Mother, and my pony needs it."

Father said, "I am making a silver bridle for your pony."

The boy answered, "I will like that. My pony will look fine with a new blanket and bridle."

The lovely wife of Elder Brother had been listening to everything. She admired the skillful weaving and the silver work of the bridle. She spoke softly to Little Singer:

"I have nothing to give you, but I know that the clouds and the stars are calling you. I think if you sing of them, you will bring them to us. Will you sing, Brother?"

"Let us sing together," said Uncle. "Let us sing a Sky song."

This is what they sang, while daylight faded away.

> *From the house made of dawn,*
> *On the trail of the dawn,*
> *He is coming to us;*
> *He is coming.*
>
> *Now the Bearer of the Day*
> *Sends a beam from the blue.*
> *It is shining on us,*
> *It is shining.*
>
> *To the house made of night,*
> *On a trail made of night,*
> *He is going from us,*
> *He is going.*

Now the Bearer of the Day
Sends the stars to the sky.
They are watching above,
They are watching.

"Yes, they are watching above, Little Singer. I can see them through the smoke hole. With your singing you have brought them to us. Now we can sleep."

The young wife of Elder Brother lay down on a sheepskin beside her sleeping baby. The beads of her silver necklace clinked when she turned on her side.

The embers of the fire paled to gray while the family slept peacefully under the watching stars.

Only Younger Brother lay awake for a while, wondering what held the stars in the sky.

CHAPTER XV

THE DARK WIND

OMETHING was making Younger Brother restless. At night he dreamed of strange experiences and new places. He dreamed of floating down a river on a raft of logs. The river grew so wide he couldn't see its other side. The water was blue, the color of turquoise. Younger Brother could feel himself gliding smoothly on the water until he hit something and awoke. Every night he had that dream of gliding in watery space until he hit something that awoke him. He never knew what it was that he hit. In the daytime he tried to reason it out and he grew restless.

He wanted to glide in the daytime and find the thing that awoke him. He knew he glided toward the west. It must be the wide water of the west that he saw in his dream. He had always wanted to go to the wide water. Perhaps if he did he could find the Turquoise Woman.

He came to think more and more about the Turquoise Woman of the western sea. Ever since he had dressed the

86

juniper stick for the girl to carry in the dance, he had dreamed of the turquoise water at night, and thought of the Turquoise Woman in the daytime.

He was terribly restless. Mother's weaving was beautiful on his pony; so was Father's bridle, but he knew the Turquoise Woman was calling him to the west. Every morning he drove the sheep toward the west. Maybe if he went far enough he could find the wide water.

He grew to hate the sheep because he must take them back toward the east every afternoon.

One morning, after awaking from his gliding dream, he told Mother he would not take the sheep out that day as he must be about other business.

"Son, are you crazy? The sheep must be herded," said Mother.

"Then you must herd them for today I travel west on my pony."

Mother looked at him and did not say a word. What she had been dreading had come to pass. Her younger son was leaving her.

She packed dried meat and corn cakes in a flour sack and tied them on his pony's saddle. She rolled a sheepskin in a blanket and tied that on.

Younger Brother put his bow and arrows in front of the saddle and was ready to leave. He shook hands with his father, merely saying:

"I ride to the west."

He put his arms around his mother, who clung to him for a moment, then said:

"When you are hungry, the mutton will be ready."

He mounted his pony and was off without once looking back at the hogan.   When out of sight and hearing he sang wildly as he rode,

The Sun Bearer travels a trail to the west,
The Moon Bearer travels a trail to the west,
Westward the stars move.   Westward move I.

The rocky cliffs answered back, "Westward move I."

The pony neighed as he scented a coyote howling on a hill. A hawk screeched as it flew toward the west.   Above the crooked rocks Yellow Beak circled in the blue.   The boy stopped his pony and called to him,

"My trail goes to the west."

He skirted the crooked rocks and rode far beyond.   By the time the Sun Bearer had reached the zenith the boy had passed the Waterless Mountain.   He never looked back.   The west was calling.

When he stopped to rest on top of a cedar ridge, he tied the pony to a tree and lay flat on his back.   Dim in the distance he could see the blue peak of the western mountain.   In the valley ahead he could trace the wash by a rolling line of dust blowing along its course.

"That means a sandstorm," he said to the pony.   "We had better move quickly to shelter."

As he rode toward the valley, which must be crossed, the storm increased. The sand blew higher in the air until it obscured the sun. The pony struggled on against the wind. The boy knew that shelter must be found. He couldn't keep his eyes open. His ears and hair were full of the fine dust. He dismounted. It was impossible for the pony to struggle further against the fury of the storm.

Younger Brother unrolled his blanket, put it over his head, and stood close to the pony as if to shelter him. The sand was blowing so thick it was like a fog enveloping them. The boy knew there was nothing to do but wait.

He could not see ten feet ahead of him. Loose tumbleweeds flew past him. Sometimes they were hurled into the air, out of sight. Sand piled up against the sagebrush and in some cases covered the lower shrubs. Clouds of dust enveloped the boy and the pony, each standing with bowed head and closed eyes, helpless before elemental fury.

Darker and darker grew the atmosphere; colder and colder, the wind. Younger Brother thought of his mother's warm hogan with the sheep skins around the fire, but he said to himself, "I must travel to the west."

While he stood there fighting the thought of the cosy family group, he was startled by a cry — a long shrill cry of despair. He could see nothing.

The cry was human. Out of the wilderness it came, adding terror to the storm. Younger Brother did not move. The pony trembled. The cry came nearer.

Younger Brother opened his eyes for a second. He could see

nothing but whirling sand and tumbleweed. He shut his eyes again and leaned close against the trembling pony.

Another cry pierced the air. It sounded nearer, much nearer. When Younger Brother opened his eyes again he could distinguish a form moving toward him.

He, too, trembled and clutched the pony's bridle to hold him. The pony reared in an effort to escape the phantom-like form in the dust. The boy's impulse was to mount and ride away but something kept him rooted to the spot.

Before he knew what was happening, the phantom figure fell at his feet. The cry was silenced. Younger Brother looked down on the limp figure of a white boy. He was dressed in khaki and wore high laced boots. His hat was missing and his blond hair curled in a tangled mass about his forehead.

Younger Brother leaned over him. The white boy looked up at the Navaho, with eyes as blue as Hasteen Tso's. He spoke the only Navaho word he knew, "Toh."

Younger Brother untied a canteen of water from the saddle and the white boy lifted it to his lips. The toh revived him. Together the two boys sat by the pony with Younger Brother's blanket about them. The wind was abating.

By sunset the dust no longer flew and the boys could see the western mountain dark against a vermilion sky. Younger Brother rolled his blanket, mounted his pony and motioned the white boy to sit behind him.

Together they rode toward the western mountain.

*Clouds of dust enveloped the boy and the pony, helpless before
elemental fury.*

CHAPTER XVI

WESTWARD BOUND

ILE after mile of gray sagebrush stretched toward the purpling mountain, the only distinctive landmark in sight.

The white boy was straining his eyes in search of a lone cottonwood where he had left his roadster early in the afternoon.

Younger Brother kept a lookout for smoke from some hogan, as he had no desire to sleep out on the desert.

The pony was the first to find a camp, for he scented water and galloped gladly toward it. Younger Brother let him have the rein and soon, around a little rise of ground, they came upon a spring. The white boy shouted with joy, as he recognized the lone cottonwood by the spring; and there was his roadster, the cause of all his trouble. It had run out of gasoline, five miles from a trading post. The boy had started to walk to the post for help, when he was overtaken by the sandstorm and lost.

He motioned to Younger Brother to dismount and the two boys proceeded to set up a tent that was stored in the back of the car. The white boy took out his pots and pans while

Younger Brother made a campfire of sagebrush. Soon the smell of coffee brewing and bacon frying made the boys realize how hungry they were.

"Gee, this is the real thing," said the white boy, as he opened a can of sardines and put two of them on a cracker.

"Have some ?" he asked the Navaho. Younger Brother shook his head, "No."

When the big yellow canned peaches were passed, they were not refused. They are not taboo for Navahos, but fish is. My ! They tasted good ! Younger Brother watched every move of his new friend. He was a big boy about fifteen and though strong and muscular, seemed tired out after his fight with the wind. That was because he had become frightened and lost his head.

After supper Younger Brother watered the pony, removed the saddle, and took the blanket and sheepskin into the tent. Then he hobbled the pony so that he couldn't wander too far away.

He gave a parting look at the western mountain all purple against the darkening sky, then went inside the tent and lay down on his sheepskin. He kept all his clothes on. He was much interested in watching the white boy unlace his boots, take off his khaki clothes and put on his white pajama suit, which looked just like the clothes the old Navaho men wore all the time in the summer, only this suit was much whiter.

He watched the boy brush his short blond hair and they both laughed at the sand that shook out of it. Then he untied the woolen string wound around the coil of his own hair and let the long black mass hang over his shoulders. He had no brush so he just ran his fingers through his hair and managed to get a lot of sand out.

The white boy watched him coil and tie his hair again. To him it seemed funny that any boy should have long hair like a girl's but he was learning many new and different things as he traveled.

The boys slept soundly all night and in the morning the white boy tried to make Younger Brother understand what he wanted to do. He pointed to the auto and he pointed down the road, said "toh" and shook his head for "no."

The Navaho boy thought he wanted water and started toward the spring with a bucket. The white boy gesticulated, "No."

Then Younger Brother had an inspiration. He said excitedly: "Jedi-be-toh. Jedi-be-toh."

Suddenly the white boy recalled that the Navahos call gasoline "jedi-be-toh." He was delighted that they understood each other. He realized that jedi meant the sound of the engine. Toh meant water and be meant its, so there was the Navaho word for gasoline — "automobile its water."

He was so delighted he shook Younger Brother's hand and pointing down the road and to the pony said, "jedi-be-toh." After a while he succeeded in making himself understood and the two started out again, riding the pony.

At the post the trader interpreted for the boys. He asked Younger Brother where he had come from.

"From the Waterless Mountain," said the boy.

"Why are you with the Pelicano?"

"The Pelicano boy was lost in the black wind. I put him on my pony. Tell the Pelicano my pony needs hay."

Half a dozen Navahos were standing around and leaning against the counter. They had never seen Younger Brother before. They thought he was a smart boy to get hay for his pony.

The trader told the white boy it was up to him to pay for hay as well as for gasoline.

"Sure thing. I expect to, but how am I to get back with this gas ?"

"Where are you heading for ?" asked the trader.

"Grand Canyon. I expect to meet my folks there."

"I'll ask the kid what he will do for you."

Younger Brother said he was riding west and if the Pelicano wanted him to he would go with him. Of course they could not pack much gasoline on the pony, but enough to get the car to the post, where the tank was filled and everything set for a western trail.

The white boy led the way in his roadster and Younger Brother followed his tracks.

As he rode alone again he noticed clouds piling in the sky. The land was strange and new to him but the sky he could always read. He said to his pony, "The voice of the thunder will be heard in the land today."

It wasn't long before drops of rain spattered in the dust and on the sagebrush. It smelled so good, so fresh, just as it smelled at home near the Waterless Mountain.

The little pony jogged along, glad of the clouds which made shade for his going. He still followed the track of the roadster.

In the distance thunder was rolling and banging. By the time Younger Brother reached a high stretch of ground, he could see the opposite side of a rocky wash streaked with blue and red and yellow. Behind the mesa dark blue-black thunder clouds spit out streaks of lightning just like the darting tongues of serpents.

Rain began to fall in torrents. It washed away the tracks of the automobile and almost washed away the road itself. The water made deep channels, leaving a terribly high center in the road. Younger Brother followed the road until it forked on top of a steep bank. Below he could see water running in the wash. What had been a dry wash an hour ago, was now a raging torrent coming down from the mountains.

He wondered if his friend had been able to cross. At the forking of the road, Younger Brother turned to the right. He had not gone more than half a mile in the drenching rain before he found the white boy and his car stuck in the sand on the edge of the wash.

Younger Brother was wet to the skin but the white boy was dry. He had sat helpless with a blanket around him, after digging for an hour in the sand. The hind wheels were in mud to the hubs.

The white boy was glad to see Younger Brother ride up, and he motioned him to jump in the car out of the wet. There they sat, waiting for the rain to stop.

After a while the sun shone again, just long enough to say goodby, with a flood of orange and magenta light dancing on the rocky cliffs. The boys proceeded to make a fire. Younger

Brother's clothes must be dried.   That was a problem as he had nothing to wear while they were drying.   The white boy loaned him a blanket and as he sat by the little campfire he could see two Navaho horsemen on the opposite bank riding fast and furiously.

They slowed up as they approached the river and consulted about crossing.   Then in Navaho fashion they dismounted, and urged their horses into the water to swim across.   Each Navaho followed his horse, holding tightly to its tail while it swam. They crossed that way all right.   Navahos are not strong on swimming.   They let the ponies do it for them.

At the camp they sat down by the fire and joined the boys in a cup of coffee.   They talked with Younger Brother and told him the machine might get lost in the night as the flood would get higher.   One of the men said:

"What if it does ?   Then the Pelicano will have to pay us for a pony."

Younger Brother looked at the fellow.   He had never met that kind of man before.   He didn't like his looks.   He had little mean eyes and a cruel mouth.

Younger Brother said nothing for a while.   He just sat, wrapped in the blanket, thinking.   He knew the machine must be hauled back onto high ground and the sooner it was done the better.   So he told the two men if they would help dig and push, the Pelicano would pay them.

"How much ?" asked the wicked-looking one.

"One peso," said Younger Brother.

"It is not enough," said the man.

"I think it is enough. It will buy much tobacco."

The white boy was helpless in this situation. He knew that it was not safe to leave his car so near the water. He guessed that the men were bargaining so he held up two fingers and said, "Pesos."

One man went to work with the shovel while the other brought sagebrush to fill up the soft muddy ruts. Younger Brother still sat wrapped in his blanket while the white boy jacked up the rear end of the car. After repeated trials of starting the engine and putting more brush in the ruts, the car was finally pulled out and off the road for the night. It was safe from the danger of a flood.

The white boy gave the men a dollar each and more coffee. As they rode away Younger Brother wished they had gone back across the water. He didn't like them and he would feel easier to have a river between himself and the men.

The white boy was in the best of spirits because his car was safe. He thought what a lucky thing it was for him that he met the Navaho boy. It was good to have someone that could talk to the natives for him. He wished he could tell the Navaho that he liked him. Of course Younger Brother knew that he did, but white people always like to talk.

While the tent was being set up for the night, Younger Brother put on his clothes. They were nearly dry and he must attend to his pony, who was grazing a little way off.

He called the pony with a low sweet whistling sound. The white boy, busy driving tent stakes, thought he heard a mourning dove calling. He didn't know that Younger Brother had taught the pony to obey that call. It had taken months to teach him but now he always answered.

The pony came up to have the saddle removed. He was a pinto pony marked with big white spots on red. A small white crescent between the eyes was the only mark on his red face.

Younger Brother took the buckskin hobble from the saddle and put it on the pony's flanks. He went off to graze in the sagebrush.

A bucket of water was brought from the wash and left to stand over night. It was so muddy that it would take all night to settle. Everything was as cosy as possible inside the little tent and for the second night the two boys lay down to sleep.

The white boy was still wishing he could talk with the Navaho. There were so many questions to ask about cliff dwellings and arrows and old pottery and hunting. He knew that the boy had a bow and arrows but he hadn't seen him use them yet. They were lying close to him with the bridle and the saddle blanket. The white boy thought the silver bridle was a beauty and he knew his mother would like to own the blanket with the red tassels on the corners.

Younger Brother didn't miss the talking. Being an Indian he found entertainment in just lying still and doing nothing. Besides he was always thinking of the wide water where the Turquoise Woman lived in her turquoise house. He was content because he was headed toward the west. He fell asleep listening to the water roaring down the wash. It too was headed west and would some day lose its red, muddy self in the wide water, where the kind mother of all lived in her turquoise house.

CHAPTER XVII

ADVENTURES OF THE PINTO

URRAY for the desert !" shouted the white boy as he turned a somersault in front of the little tent.

"Hurray for the coffee and bacon," he called, and turned another somersault.

Younger Brother stopped poking the sagebrush fire to watch the antics of his friend. He supposed he was performing some morning ceremony of the whites. Maybe it was his way of greeting the sun. Probably it was, for the whole valley shimmered in the glory of early sunlight. Everything was fresh and clean, washed by the rain of yesterday.

The air was invigorating and pungent with the smell of wet sagebrush. The swishing sound of water rose from the wash, which was still flooded from the cloudbursts of the previous day.

The white boy knew he could not ford the stream for some time, so after breakfast he motioned to Younger Brother to go for the pony, indicating that he would clean camp, pack the car, and stay by the saddle.

So Younger Brother started out to follow the clear hoofprints in the damp sand. They led into the brush where the pony had grazed.

Probably he wasn't far away. He never wandered too far from camp. For about a mile the boy walked, when he noticed the traces of two more horses. Still there was no sight of his pony.

Examining the tracks he realized that they were made by the horses of the two Navahos who had helped to dig the roadster out of the mud. He was alarmed for he could tell by his pony's tracks that the hobbles had been removed.

With great anxiety he followed the marks back to the road he had traveled the day before. At a lone cedar tree the tracks led to the left and entered the brushy ground again.

Younger Brother was discouraged. Following on foot was slow but he kept on with only one thought. He must find his pony. On and on he trudged until he came to the edge of a deep gully made by the water from heavy rains.

Looking down the gully he saw a thin blue smoke rising above the far side of a bend. Carefully and quietly he walked in its direction, keeping on the crest of the bank. When he was ready to turn the bend, he hid in the bushes and listened.

He could hear the two Navahos talking. One was saying, "The pony will bring thirty pesos."

"Who will buy it ? No one has thirty pesos."

"If no one buys him, I, myself will ride him."

"Yes, you say you will ride him but what shall I ride then ?"

"As you ride now."

"Half of that pony is mine. We worked together."

Younger Brother listened in wrath. That was his pony. Uncle had given it to him and he had trained it to do his will through the long days of sheep herding. They were the closest of friends. No one should steal the pony from him. No one could. He would get him back.

He crawled stealthily among the bushes until he was directly above the campfire of the horse thieves. He could see his pony with the two horses of the Navahos. He looked so beautiful, with the white crescent shining on his forehead and the pattern of big white-and-red spots marking the rounded grace of his body. He was not tied and was nibbling a few stray blades of grass on the margin of the gully.

Younger Brother crawled noiselessly through the brush to reach the windward side of the pony. There was just a little stir in the pure air and he figured it would carry the scent of him to his pony.

After a little while of patient waiting, he saw the pony lift his nose and sniff. Then he whinnied a little and pricked up his ears. The horse thieves noticed the actions and one of them said, "What does he hear?"

"Nothing," said the other. "I hear nothing."

The pony decided to graze again, moving in the direction of Younger Brother. The two Navahos resumed their quarreling and while they were talking Younger Brother breathed his own special note of the mourning dove.

Immediately the pony ran toward the sound, whinnying as he went. He started right up the wet sandy bank of the gully.

In his haste he dislodged big chunks of dirt, precipitating a small landslide.

The horse thieves jumped to their saddles to pursue. Younger Brother trembled with excitement as he saw them start toward the bank.

Again he whistled the mourning dove note and he could see his pony leap to the top of the bank. His head was held high and his nostrils distended.

Another big piece of dirt fell from behind him, uprooting a yucca plant which rolled down the bank, landing in the path of the horse thieves.

Younger Brother remained hidden, expecting to be discovered at any minute. He was alert, waiting for the right moment to emerge from the bushes. He could not see the thieves.

Suddenly he heard them yell in terror. They were calling "Chindi, chindi, ghost," and as the boy peeked out from behind the bush he could see the two rascals riding up the opposite bank as fast as their horses could carry them.

Younger Brother was amazed. He wondered what had frightened them. Maybe they had seen his eyes peering through the bushes. He didn't know what the dislodged yucca plant had uncovered. From the top of the bank he couldn't see the prehistoric grave with its beautiful big pottery jar standing beside an ancient skeleton.

The thieves had seen it and they were horrified. They had no desire to own a pony who must be chindi himself. Why had he whinnied and looked in the direction of the grave? He must have known it was there.

Younger Brother wondered what had frightened them.

So the thieves rode away frightened out of their wits.

Younger Brother walked boldly to the edge of the bank and looked over. He could see the beautiful jar, so big it would take both of his arms to reach around it.

He would like to take it to the white boy but, when he ran down the bank and saw the bones, he wouldn't touch the jar. He knew it belonged to the ancient people. Uncle had always told him to leave such things alone.

So he went up the bank and mounted his pony, happy to have him again. He rode bareback to camp, where he found the white boy rather anxious.

Younger Brother was excited and tried to tell his story with gestures. He could not make himself understood.

By this time the water had gone down in the wash, so that it was safe for the roadster to cross. Younger Brother rode his pony in to test the bottom. It was rocky, so there was no fear of quicksand.

Once more the boys were westward bound. They stopped at the next trading post for gasoline. The trader was good-natured and allowed them to camp near the store and put the pony in the corral with a good supper of hay.

The boys spent the evening with the trader in his living room. It was a splendid big stone-walled room with Navaho blankets hanging on the walls and piled half way to the ceiling in one end of the room. The floor was carpeted with the blankets. A big stone fireplace suggested cosy evenings in the winter time.

The white boy asked the trader to find out what had hap

pened to his Navaho friend that morning, and Younger Brother told about the horse thieves.

"They tried to steal my pony," he said.

"What did they look like, my boy ?"

"Like the spittle of snakes, like dried coyotes, like chindi."

"Hard to identify," said the trader. "Try again."

"One was squint-eyed, with a mouth that could kill."

"Sounds like Cut Finger. He's a bad egg," said the trader, turning to the white boy. "The government's looking for him. How did you get the pony back, boy ?"

"He came when I called him."

"Well, well, as easy as that !" laughed the trader. "What became of the thieves ?"

"They rode to the north when my pony found the pot and the bones."

"Found what pot, what bones ?"

"The big red pot with the black snake on the outside."

The trader was excited by this time. "How big was the pot ?"

"So big my arms could not reach around it."

"Will you show me the place tomorrow ?"

"No, I must travel to the west. It is not good to disturb the ancient people."

Nothing could induce Younger Brother to guide the trader to the place of the pot.

The white boy was excited about the pot because his father was an archaeologist looking for old things. He decided to investigate for himself. He wanted to find the pot.

So the next morning he and Younger Brother parted company. He gave the Navaho boy a dollar for a present and watched him ride his pinto pony into the west.

Younger Brother was again free to dream of the wide water. He couldn't help feeling a bit homesick as he rode past hogans or watched a flock of sheep herded by some child; but coupled with the feeling of homesickness was the urge to be free.

CHAPTER XVIII

SECRETS TO SHARE

OUNGER BROTHER'S spirits rose as he traveled. He was unhampered by any routine duty. It was such a relief to be freed from sheep herding. The pony could graze at night and the boy could hunt for rabbits when he needed them. He still had dried meat in the flour sack. The corn cakes were gone, but he could always stop at a hogan if he wished. There he would be welcome.

With no material thing to worry about, he had time to dream to his heart's content as he journeyed toward the west.

At times he was lonely, but not for any particular person. The loneliness came when he was the happiest. Then he felt the old longing to share his joy with someone, as he had wanted to share the secret of the cave when he was a little boy.

He had other secrets now which he wanted to share, but they were such sacred secrets he was sure no one but the Turquoise Woman would understand them. She had understood the loneliness of the White Shell Woman when the waterfall was

calling. He was sure she could understand him. He was puzzled about all the things that were happening inside of him.

The songs of birds made him run to the hilltops. The hilltops made him sing when he felt like crying. The sage-
scented wind made him sigh and when he touched the soft
nose of his pony, a shivery joy ran all through his body.

He remembered all the beautiful things of the past — the
deer dancing in the sunlight, the bumblebee and the pollen,
the tail feathers of Yellow Beak, the deep, deep pool. Most of
all he remembered the wand he had dressed for the girl to
carry in the dance of the maidens.

Uncle had told him that the wand had something to do with
the Turquoise Woman. He remembered the story of her
journey to the west and he liked to think that he was traveling
the same trail.

The Sun Bearer had urged her to travel west, because he
loved her and wanted her to make a home for him there.
They had discussed the subject while they sat on top of one of
the seven sacred mountains, and she had told the Sun Bearer
that she did not like to leave her sister and her sons. She asked,
"Why should I move to a strange place where I should be alone
all day ?"

He answered, "Your boys told me you would go."

"I am not bound by the promise of my sons. I am a woman
of freedom, who speaks for herself."

"But I want you to go to the west," pleaded the Sun Bearer.
"I want you for my own."

"No, no, no, no," said the beautiful Turquoise Woman.

The fifth time that the Sun Bearer begged her to make a home for him, she said, "Well, what kind of home would it be ? I know that you have a good house in the east. I have heard about it."

"It is a beautiful house," said the Sun Bearer.

"Mine must be more beautiful," said the Turquoise Woman.

The Sun Bearer smiled. He felt sure that he was winning her. She continued, "My house must float on the western water, away from the shore, because I do not want everyone visiting me. Certain people annoy me."

"It shall float on the water as you wish, oh, Woman of Turquoise."

"And I want white shells, turquoise, abalone shells, jet, soap-stone, agate, and red stones all around my house."

"You shall have all that you wish, my Woman of Turquoise."

"I have not yet said I am your Woman of Turquoise," she answered. "I am myself and free."

The Sun Bearer smiled and the whole earth was warmed. Even the woman by his side became less cold.

She said, "If I go to the west I shall be lonely. I shall long for my sister and my sons. Could you make pets for me to take along ?"

"Surely," he promised. "I will make elk, buffalo, deer and long-tail deer."

"That will not be enough, oh, Bearer of the Day."

The Sun Bearer looked at her. She was the loveliest thing in creation. He knew he could produce anything for her sake, so he promised to make mountain sheep, jack rabbits and prairie dogs.

"Will that satisfy you?" he asked.

"I think I shall manage for a while," she said.

So in time she started westward with all her animals. The Mirage People and the Ground Heat People went with her to help drive the animals.

They stopped at different places for ceremonies. In the Black Mountain country the buffalos stampeded. They didn't like mountain country, so they stamped and tramped on the mountain till they made a big pass, and then they ran away back east. They stayed in the east always.

Some of the antelope and deer ran east too. Later the elks went back. All of them went back. They never returned to the Turquoise Woman in the west.

When the party arrived at the western mountain, a ceremony was held for the Turquoise Woman. She lay on top of the mountain with her head to the west. The Mirage People molded her body till it was perfect. Then they sang songs of her perfection.

After they left the western mountain to journey to the wide water, they followed a trail that nobody knows today. After long hard travel over deserts where water was scarce, they reached the western water. There the Turquoise Woman could see her floating house shimmering in the smile of the Sun Bearer.

It was as beautiful as she had wished, all made of turquoise and so high that its upper story was lost in the clouds.

The waves of the wide water sang a welcome to the Turquoise Woman, as she entered her new home.

The first thing she did was to build a fire so her husband would feel at home when he came bearing the sun.

Younger Brother, thinking of this story as he rode through the sagebrush, could see the western mountain far in the distance. The sight of it gave him courage to ride on during the long hot days. At night by the light of his campfire, he carved from a piece of cottonwood, the prayer stick he intended to offer to the western mountain.

The secret joy inside of him responded to the joy of all the desert world and he knew that the holy ones watched him from the heat waves and the mirage which danced before his eyes. They had helped the Turquoise Woman in her journey to the west and they would help him.

CHAPTER XIX

BEAUTIFUL UNDER THE COTTONWOODS

IN THE freshness of a quiet desert morning, when no sound but the mocking-bird's call is heard, it is good to take stock of blessings. So thought Younger Brother, lying wrapped in his blanket under the summer shelter of his newest friend.

He had spent the night with a family of his own clan. The woman of the place was a distant relative of his mother. "Beautiful under the Cottonwoods," she called her home. A real river ran past it. In the summer-time corn fields flourished on its banks, due to the ease of irrigating.

Younger Brother could see the green tasseled corn from where he lay. The soil was rich with the silt of many overflows.

The woman at this camp was a widow with two daughters. She had decided to marry again, and hoped she would be acceptable to the brother of her late husband.

For days she had ground corn and made the thin corn bread the Navahos like so well. When Younger Brother had ridden to her camp the night before, he had found her spreading **the** thin batter on a hot rock. He had watched her roll the paper-thin sheets as she removed them from her primitive stove.

She told him that in the morning she would carry the bread and the meal in two baskets to the home of her brother-in-law.

As Younger Brother listened to the song of the mocking-bird, he watched his relative prepare for her quest. She was a good-looking woman dressed in a dark blue velveteen jacket and a black skirt. The ends of her red woolen sash hung down the side with a few little sea shells tied to the fringe.

She carried her baskets of corn meal and paper bread. On top of the baskets she had formed a cross of wild grape vines. Younger Brother wondered where she had found the vine. She must have ridden a long way for that.

He hoped she would have good luck in finding a husband. She would place the baskets a short distance from the hogan where her brother-in-law lived. If he were willing to marry her, his family would eat the meal and the bread and in four days he would go to the widow's house.

Younger Brother decided to stay with his relative to see what would happen. His pony could rest and graze and it was pleasant for the boy to be with his young cousins. They were glad to hear about his adventures and he felt like quite a hero as he told of his wanderings.

At sunset of the fourth day the family waited inside the hogan. Everything was ready for the hoped-for husband. Younger Brother was thinking any good man should be glad to marry his relative. She was a fine weaver and owned a large flock of sheep.

He was not surprised when he heard the dogs barking outside and saw the blanket lifted from the doorway, but he was surprised at the beauty and youth of the naked man who entered. He wore only his loin cloth. In his hand he carried a bow and arrows, which he put by the woman sitting in the west.

Younger Brother had never seen such a splendid-looking man. He was tall and straight and smooth skinned. Surely he was worthy of the wife he was accepting.

He stayed all night in the hogan and the following morning he and the woman washed in a bowl of yucca suds. Then they combed each other's long black hair. The woman looked happy and contented. The home near the river was complete now, with a man to cook and weave for.

The holy ones should have looked down in approval on the happy family, but something very terrible was happening in the skies. The sun itself was sick. A shadow crept over it, bringing fear into every Navaho heart.

Every Indian in the country stopped his work or his journey to sit in silence watching the death of the orb. Younger Brother sang a song of blessing that his uncle had taught him, and a neighboring medicine man hurried to make a sand painting of the sun.

He drew it on the ground outside the hogan. It was a blue disk outlined with the sacred colors. Forty-eight rays of light were drawn around it, allowing twelve of every one of the four colors for every cardinal direction.

That was to give the Sun Bearer courage as he carried the dying sun. He could look down and know that the people of the earth were helping him with their perfect pictures of the sun.

The air grew cold. Shadows of the cottonwood leaves made a double outline on the ground. Soon all the earth was in shadow. A few chickens went to roost in the cottonwoods. The Navahos were still. Little by little the shadow passed from the sun. A rooster crowed as he would at dawn. The sun was well. The eclipse was over. Again the Sun Bearer traveled a trail of beauty to the west.

Younger Brother felt extremely sober. He feared disaster. The last time that darkness covered the sun, the people of the earth had suffered from a very bad sickness. Many had died from heat in the head.

That night while Younger Brother slept in the summer shelter, he was awakened by wind and rain, which forced him to join the family inside the hogan. His relative was awake and worried.

She said, "Why should we have such a storm this time of year ? Always when the Sun sickens there is trouble."

"Yes, Mother, that is what my uncle has told me."

"Your uncle should tell you how to make peace with the storm people."

The boy thought of the time he had sprinkled pollen on the clouds. He thought of Hasteen Tso and the song they had sung together when they flew in the giant dragon-fly.

He felt very much alone. He missed Uncle. He missed Mother. He almost forgot the Turquoise Woman.

His relative put a wash tub under the smoke hole. Too

much water was coming in. The little girls slept soundly through all the noise. So did the new man of the house.

All night the storm raged. In the morning the sky hung gray and heavy. The Sun Bearer did not leave his home in the east. Instead he sent the evil serpents of lightning across the sky.

. Day after day no sun shone on the people of the earth, and the water continued to fall from the clouds. The red muddy river rose higher and higher.

The family in the hogan could look from the doorway and see bits of wreckage floating down the river. Logs and up-rooted trees whirled past.

Prairie dogs, rabbits, snakes came out of their holes and traveled past the hogan to higher land.

The woman feared for her hogan. She asked her husband to help her move her household goods. The rain ceased for a while and the sun sent a feeble ray of light to shine on the hogan by the river.

Higher and higher the water rose. Sheep were floating down the muddy torrent. The woman feared for her flock. She started to drive them to the little rise of ground where the prairie dogs and the snakes had gone.

Bit by bit the water was eating away the bank by the corn fields. Everyone worked packing the household goods to the brushy hill a mile away.

Younger Brother helped the two little girls to carry their mother's loom. All the afternoon the family struggled. By night time the green growing corn was all washed away and swept down the river.

Still the muddy water rose higher and higher. All night the family struggled to save its wealth. The beautiful young husband tried to drive the frantic sheep through two feet of water. In the darkness he worked in vain. Most of the sheep were lost.

Younger Brother waited on the hill with his cousins. He tried to make a fire. Everything was too wet to burn. With the woman's help he managed to make a little shelter with the poles from the loom and what sheepskins they had saved.

Toward dawn the beautiful young husband staggered to the camp with half a dozen bleating sheep. He sank to the ground exhausted. All night he had been in the water. He was shivering. There was no fire, no hot coffee, no dry clothes.

The clouds were gone and the evil serpents of lightning no longer crossed the sky. The Bearer of the Day appeared in the east and looked down upon the destruction.

Younger Brother managed to get a fire started. He had enough water in his canteen to make the coffee. By the time the sun was high enough to dry things out a bit, the handsome young man was burning with fever. The struggle had been too much for him.

In two days he died of "no lungs" — pneumonia. His wife was dazed. When the water went down she walked to "Beautiful under the Cottonwoods." Slippery red mud covered everything. The few bedraggled chickens were huddled on top of the hogan.

Inside it was a sorry sight, with slushy mud a foot deep. She

She threw the bow and arrows in with these words, "Tieholtsodi, monster of the waters, take these also."

walked to the west side and took from a niche between the logs, a bow and arrows. They were the symbols of her second marriage. She walked to the river and leaning over the red muddy water, threw the bow and arrows in with these words:

"Tieholtsodi, monster of the waters, take these also. You have taken my sheep, my corn, and my husband."

With a little gurgling sound the water monster swallowed the bow and arrows.

The woman was alone, with two little girls to care for, and only six sheep left for her support.

"Beautiful under the Cottonwoods" was no longer beautiful.

CHAPTER XX

THE WESTERN MOUNTAIN

OR FOUR days the widow and her two little girls fasted and mourned for the loss of the man of their house. The fast was not required of Younger Brother because he had not been present at the death.

He had ridden to the home of a neighbor for help. There he found kindly people who offered shelter to the widow until she could arrange her affairs.

Younger Brother decided the old hogan must be moved to higher ground, so with the help of the neighbors it was taken apart and the logs hauled in a wagon to a site beyond reach of another overflow. A corral for the sheep was built of driftwood from the flood. The sheep were the widow's only property. The horses that were saved were inherited by the relatives of her husband. His favorite riding horse had been saddled and shot beside his grave, so that he might have a mount in the spirit world.

Younger Brother felt that he must resume his journey. He had been two weeks with his relative. The woman begged him to stay. She had grown to love him as a son. Besides he was such a help to her in her poverty. He told her that he had left his own mother and he could remain no longer. He must be traveling to the west.

"What is it that you seek in the west ?" the woman asked. "Have you ever seen it or heard it ?"

"No, Mother."

"Foolish boy. Why do you leave two mothers and ride to the west ?"

"Because I must see the wide water."

"Is there not enough water here ? Think how cruel the water has been to me." As she spoke the woman eloquently pointed to the desolate fields.

The boy had been thinking about it and he said, "Tieholtsodi claims his own. The water monster cannot forget that the coyote stole his children."

"That was in the beginning, child, and has naught to do with us."

Younger Brother again spoke, "I am not wise like Uncle. He could make you understand that all that has gone before has much to do with us."

The two were sitting outside the newly-finished hogan. From its higher position, it commanded a view of the valley, stretching its gray waste far to the mesa country. The sunlit river glistened as it sinuously moved westward.

A black spot appeared in the distance and Younger Brother realized that an automobile was traveling in their direction. As it came nearer he recognized the roadster of the white boy.

He ran to stop the machine. The Navaho woman went inside the hogan.

The white boy was surprised to see Younger Brother and he couldn't help talking even though he were not understood. He jumped out of the car saying, "Hello, there. I'm glad to see you're not drowned out. We've all had an awful time back there."

The two boys entered the hogan where the woman hospitably made some coffee. She had very little else to offer. The boy noticed this and by signs learned something of the tragedy caused by the flood.

He left some canned goods with the woman and bought a rug that she had saved from the wreck of her home. When Younger Brother helped to pack the rug in the back of the roadster, he noticed a large burlap-covered package. His friend took it out to rewrap carefully. Younger Brother's keen eyes recognized the shape of a big pot.

He stopped packing, for instinctively he knew the white boy had found what he had stayed behind to find — the big red pot with the black snake pictured on the outside.

Younger Brother had no desire to touch it nor to see it. The white boy made no move to show it to him for he understood the sacredness of the ancient relic.

He was secretly elated at his success in finding the pot and was hurrying to get word to his father at Grand Canyon, for he thought he had discovered some unknown ruins buried in the sand.

The flood had washed away much more soil from the bank

where the pony had found the pot and there were signs of stone walls, much chipped flint, and broken bits of pottery.

After the white boy left in his car, Younger Brother sat inside the hogan, thinking hard. He was trying to put two and two together. He said to himself, "First my pony finds the pot. Next the white boy finds it. Then comes the shadow on the Sun. Then comes the storm and the flood and the death of the beautiful young husband."

Younger Brother continued his thinking. He couldn't understand. If Uncle were only here he could help with his wisdom. He went on with his puzzling. He thought about the snake painted on the outside of the pot. It was one of the holy people who guarded the secrets of the underworld.

The snake must have told the Sun Bearer about the grave being disturbed. Probably that made the Sun sicken. But why must the handsome young husband die ?

Younger Brother was not wise enough to fathom that. The harder he thought and puzzled, the worse matters became. If Uncle were only there he would help him to understand. How he wished Uncle were with him.

He stopped puzzling his brain to remember Uncle's kind, serious face, lit with the joy of the songs he sang. He could almost hear the songs of beauty.

Suddenly he remembered that he himself had not been singing in his heart. He had been too busy helping the woman to save her few possessions. That was why he couldn't understand.

He ran outside and saddled his pony.   He rode away, leaving the woman and her two little girls watching sadly from the doorway.

As his pony ran in the brilliant sunshine, Younger Brother looked with joy upon the western mountain, which now seemed very close.   Soon he would be able to place the prayer stick upon its summit.

Again his heart sang and he understood.   All his thinking could not make him understand, but his singing heart could. He called to the mountain, "Those people are earthbound. They heap too many goods.   They have not learned the trail of beauty.   They have never flown to the clouds."

He was himself again, accepting whatever came without questioning.   Never again would he forget Uncle's teachings. He would travel the trail of beauty to the west.   He would find the turquoise water.   He knew he would find it.

He was so near the western mountain he could see the pine trees on its slope.   Shafts of light streamed from behind silvery clouds marking a pathway on the mica-spattered sand for Younger Brother to travel on.   He no longer questioned.   He only sang in the silvery light.

By nightfall he was under the pines.   He lay down on the sweet dry leaves of the forest and watched the moon paint with silver light, the forms of rocks and tree trunks and sloping ground.   And while he watched, four shadowy figures moved among the trees.   The moon with its magic light made them into the shapes of the Deer People.

Younger Brother lay perfectly still as one by one the Deer

People walked past him, so close he could smell their pine-scented hoofs. He fell asleep, singing in his heart a song of rainbow land, where bright-plumaged birds built their nests in the antlers of the deer.

CHAPTER XXI

EXIT THE PINTO, ENTER THE FIRE HORSE

N THE morning when Younger Brother awoke, he knew he was in a land of enchantment. A spotted fawn arched its long neck to reach the juicy leaves above its head. It stood knee deep in tender green bracken bordering a running stream where a doe drank from the crystal purity.

Younger Brother had never been in a country of many springs. He was used to the Waterless Mountain. Uncle had told him the legends of the western mountain with its forests and little streams. He knew there was an old stone wall somewhere in the neighborhood, built by the very early clans traveling from the west to the desert country.

Soon after sunrise he started to ride his pony up the mountain trail. By noontime he reached the rocky top. He lay down with his head pointing to the west as the Turquoise Woman had done.

The sun shone warmly on his body. The ground heat and the mirage shimmered in the valley below. He was happy being on top of the world. It was almost as good as being in the clouds. It was just the kind of place to make him feel the queer pain of beauty and the need of sharing his inner secret. He wondered if there were anyone in the whole world who felt as he felt.

He took from a bag the prayer stick he had made. He tied two feathers of the yellow warbler on the stick and placed it under a shelving rock. He spoke these words, "Oh, Bearer of the Day, help me to follow the trail of beauty to the west. Grant that I may reach the wide waters."

From the little buckskin medicine bag that Uncle had given him he took a pinch of pollen, touched it to his tongue and his head, and threw the rest to the sky. Having made his offering from the summit of the western mountain, he rode back down the trail to camp for the night.

The next morning, after following a path through the pines for a mile or two, he found the wide road leading to the west. He had never seen such a wide smooth road.

Many automobiles whizzed past him, going in both directions. He was confused. Why was everyone riding so fast, some east, some west? He wondered if they were all going to the wide water or had been there. His pony was as uncomfortable as he. The whizzing cars made him nervous.

Younger Brother watched every machine, hoping that he might see the Big Man. He knew that he often drove in this direction to visit his store at the railroad.

The boy decided to rest from his riding for a while. He threw the reins over his pony's head and sat down under a scraggly juniper tree a few feet off the road. Car after car rolled by, but one stopped near the juniper tree.

A white person jumped out, carrying a little black box in her hands. Younger Brother did not know that the person was a woman, because she wore no skirts. She was dressed like a man. She pointed the black box at the boy. He heard a clicking noise and the white person looked pleased. She waved to the driver in the car and said something.

Then she moved nearer Younger Brother and pointed to his pony, saying something in a thin voice not like a man's voice. He wondered what the Pelicano wanted. Again she pointed to the pony. He pointed to the pony. He was confused.

In the meantime another car stopped. Younger Brother had not noticed it but the driver's keen eyes had recognized the pinto pony and the Navaho boy. The Big Man had arrived. He watched the tourist woman pointing to the pony's blanket and saying, "How much ?"

In Navaho he spoke to the boy:

"She wants to buy your pony's saddle blanket. I will tell her it is not for sale."

Younger Brother jumped to his feet and ran to the Big Man's car. They shook hands and smiled at each other. When the tourist car drove away, the Big Man asked, "Where are you going ?"

"To the wide water, Grandfather."

"Well, get on your pony and follow my car to the store, I will go as slowly as I can. It is not far."

Younger Brother had no trouble keeping the car in sight

until the highway reached the little Arizona town where the store was located. Then there were so many things to look out for, and so many new things to observe, he almost lost the car as it turned a corner.

He certainly was relieved when the Big Man parked in front of the store and told him to tie his pony to a hitching post. They walked upstairs to the front door.

Inside Younger Brother saw the biggest room he had ever seen in his life. One end was piled to the ceiling with rugs. There were rugs everywhere, on the floor and the walls.

He didn't know there were so many weavings in all the world. He thought there were too many. When he and the Big Man sat down on a pile of rugs to talk, he told him what he thought. He said:

"Grandfather, aren't you afraid to heap so many goods?"

The Big Man looked at him in astonishment, because he had been thinking he was overstocked, but how could this child of the wilderness know that?

"I think I have heaped too many rugs," he answered. "Now tell me what you have been doing."

"I have been riding to the west on my pony. Cut Finger stole him, but I called him back and he found a big red pot of the Ancients. The Pelicano who came in the black wind took the pot out of its resting place. Then the Sun died and I sang a song of blessing at the hogan of my relative. The Sun was restored in beauty, but the evil serpents sent the storm.

"The flood rose and swept away the sheep of my relative. Her new husband died of no lungs. I do not yet know why he must die. After that I rode to the top of the western mountain. I left my prayer stick there. Now I am here, Grandfather."

"I am glad you are here, child, for I need you. I too am traveling to the west. I am taking your mother and father and little sister on the train which the fire horse pulls. We go in four days to the place of many hogans to show the Pelicanos how to weave beauty. You shall go with us."

"Must I ride in the train behind the fire horse, Grandfather?"

"Yes, my child."

"You will be with me?"

"Yes, my child."

"Then I shall go, but what shall I do with my pony?"

"I will send him back for Uncle to care for while we are away."

"What shall I do without a pony in the place of many hogans?"

"You ask questions too fast. Did we not fly together to the clouds?"

"That is right, Grandfather. With you I doubt nothing. What you do, I shall do. Only this, Grandfather, I must tell you. . ."

The little boy leaned toward his friend and raising his big brown eyes to meet the blue eyes, said:

"My heart sings about the wide water and the floating home of the Turquoise Woman. Always I have wished to follow her trail to the west."

"We will go, my child, but remember you mustn't run away again."

The Sun Bearer and the Turquoise Woman.

"I shall not run away when you go where I wish to go. My Uncle needs water from the western sea. He needs it for his ceremonies."

Looking around the big store where Indian pottery vied with Indian baskets, Younger Brother's eyes discovered a conical jar of wicker work, glazed with pine gum.

"We need that Paiute jar, Grandfather. Always my people bring water from the west in such a jar."

"Very well, we will take the Paiute wicker jar. Now we go to the house of my sister to sleep."

CHAPTER XXII

BY THE WIDE WATERS OF THE WEST

HE BIG MAN'S sister was in town helping him prepare for the trip to the coast. She took charge of Younger Brother. She made him a beautiful purple velveteen shirt and dark green pantaloons. From the store she borrowed an old belt with eight silver disks strung on rawhide and fastened with a silver buckle of intricate design. When the boy donned his new clothes the Big Man's sister was well satisfied with her planning. She said, "We will wait for your mother to brush and tie your hair."

The thought of his mother again brushing his hair was very pleasant to Younger Brother. He was glad his family also was going to the wide water.

When Father and Mother and Sister arrived in the little town, they met the boy in the big store. They had not expected to see him and their surprise filled them with joy. The mother looked at the tall slim figure clad in purple and green and silver. She was secretly proud of him but she said, "Has no one brushed your hair?"

She immediately untied a flour sack that held her belongings and produced a Navaho hair brush. While she brushed and tied his hair, she told the boy all the news of home.

Uncle was to look after things while she was away. Elder Brother and his wife would care for the sheep. Little Sister had cried when she left the baby.

"I do not care to leave my sheep but the Big Man has asked me to weave for the Pelicanos."

"He knows what is right, Mother. My father, does he go also ?"

"Yes, he will show his silver work and your sister will be with us. Tell me, son, have you had plenty of food as you traveled ?"

"Yes, but no mutton like yours, Mother."

"There is no better mutton than mine."

The mother smiled and her even white teeth gave evidence of good food.

"There, your hair is tied. Did you meet my relative at Beautiful under the Cottonwoods ?"

"Yes, she had much trouble and lost her sheep and her young husband."

"I did not know of the young husband. What was he like ?"

"I think he was too beautiful. I think that is why he died."

"It may be so, my son. Things must not be perfect nor overdone."

"I know, Mother. Do you think the Big Man has heaped too many rugs ?" The boy waved his arm in the direction of the piles of rugs.

"No, he did not weave them himself and he does not keep them. That is all right. What is the noise I hear?"

"That is the fire horse of the Pelicanos. Tomorrow we ride in the train that the fire horse pulls."

"I do not like the fire horse."

Little Sister was frightened by the noise. She clung to her mother's long full skirt. Father was curious and wanted to see the train but dared not go outside the store.

In the morning the party left on the train. As they rode through miles of wilderness they thought it an easy way to get over the country. When the darkness came they were very tired and sleepy. They dozed in their seats all night and everyone wished he could lie on his sheepskin on the hogan floor.

Crossing the Mojave desert the next day was very tedious, but Younger Brother, looking out of the window, was glad he did not have to ride his pony across so many miles.

When the travelers finally reached the coast, the Big Man took the Navaho family to the home of a very dear friend of his, who lived in a canyon of oak trees not far from the beach.

Late in the afternoon Younger Brother and the Big Man went down to the sea carrying the Paiute jar. They walked across the sands to the sound of breaking waves.

The crash and boom of the breakers rolling in unremitting zeal upon the passive shore terrified the desert-born child. To him there was no surety of the water staying in the sea. It seemed to be making a determined effort to engulf the land.

It was like a terrible beast foaming at the mouth and hungering to devour whatever came within its reach.

Although Younger Brother was frightened by the breaking waves, the blue expanse beyond fascinated him. In the hazy distance he could see the dim outline of an island peak whose crest was lost in the clouds.

Standing close to the Big Man, the boy said, with a frightened voice, "That must be where the turquoise house is."

"It may well be there, my child."

The breakers left patterns of white foam on the wet sands, and little pools of still water. Younger Brother was filled with awe at the noise of the restless sea. He did not forget that he had often dreamed of this moment and had traveled far to attain it.

Frightened as he was, he walked toward the breaking waves. He took his medicine bag from his pocket and before sprinkling the pollen, said boldly:

"I am not afraid of you, wide water! Take this to the Turquoise Woman."

From his buckskin bag he withdrew the turquoise bead that the Big Man had left in the treasure cave, so many years ago. He blew on it. Four times he blew, and tossed it into the water with these words:

"Estsanatlehi! Changing Woman! Turquoise Woman! There is my offering from the Waterless Mountain. Restore all in beauty for my people."

The offering made, Younger Brother prepared to fill the wicker jar. He did not remove his moccasins and wade into the water. He dug a hole in the sand and let the waves fill it. Then as the water receded he filled his jar from the pool left in the hole.

"Now," he said, "my uncle will have what Estsanatlehi wishes for her children — water from her western home."

The two friends sat down on the dry sands to watch the waves roll one after another out of the wide water of the west. The sun was nearing the horizon. It sent warm, loving rays to rest for a moment on the amber-colored hills, turning their dim beauty to burning copper splendor.

The sea unrolled wave after wave of purple, tipped with orange light, until a blue mist rose from its depth. The blue mist moved across the waters and mounted to the sky.

Younger Brother watched intently. The mist mounted in swirling grace, reaching out long turquoise arms to enfold the sun as it neared its western home.

Younger Brother knew that the Sun Bearer had reached the home of the Turquoise Woman, and hung the sun on the turquoise peg in the turquoise wall. He could hear it go, "Tla, tla, tla, tla," as it settled in place.

He could not see the little gasoline fishing-boat on the other side of the wharf, seeking its harbor for the night. Its engine was stilled. The sun was resting and darkness crept over the wide water.

Younger Brother and the Big Man walked back to the house among the oaks. They found Father and Mother and Sister quite at home in front of a big fireplace.

The Big Man's friend, whom they were visiting, was a curator of the Santa Barbara museum and he was deeply interested in Indian legends. He kept his own precious finds in this room, and Father was much interested in a pair of mountain sheep horns which hung over the fireplace.

Everyone sat on the floor in Navaho fashion and ate a good meal. After that the Big Man asked Younger Brother to tell the story of the western home of the Turquoise Woman.

So while they all sat by the fire watching the particles of soot glowing and dying on the sides of the chimney, Younger Brother spoke in a dreamy voice:

"When Estsanatlehi traveled the trail of beauty to the west, she was thinking all of the way, 'Will my floating house be beautiful?' When she reached the very edge of the water and saw it sparkling from the light of the sun, she knew that her house would fulfill her heart's desire. She called to the Sun to ask him how she was to cross the water to her island home, and he sent a gorgeous rainbow for her to travel on.

"She walked gladly across the rainbow and found her beautiful house made of all the glistening stones. It was a high, two-story house, and the water came to the very edge of it.

"On the hill which rose above it, cane cactus grew very close together. Great rocks rose back of the cactus ready to crush any traveler."

Younger Brother paused in the relation of the story and the Big Man translated for his friend. The curator listened eagerly to every detail. He became more excited every minute as the description of the island was continued.

Finally he said, "This is an amazing narrative. How do

Navahos from the inland deserts know about the Channel Islands ?"

The Big Man answered, "The boy is only telling an age-old legend. Let him proceed."

Younger Brother was gazing intently into the fire. The excitement of having reached the wide water made him imaginative and happy. He turned to the Big Man and said solemnly, "I have seen the wide water of the west. I have made my offering. I have filled my jar for Uncle. My heart sings and I can see light coming from the hearth of the Turquoise Woman."

He leaned forward, looking into the fire. The pupils of his eyes dilated and his breath came fast as he spoke again, "Blue smoke rises from her fire to the sky hole. Her house glitters and shines in the sunshine. The boiling sands foam about its base.

"I can see the four mountains about the house. The Turquoise Woman has gone to the northern mountain to dance for corn and animals."

The Big Man listened in wonder. The boy continued, "Now she goes to the western mountain to dance for beautiful plants and trees. I can see the trees, Grandfather, and I can see the flowers in her hands. Grandfather, I can see her !"

Younger Brother looked up at his friend. The expression on the boy's face was like nothing the Big Man had ever seen. He was awed by the radiance of the smile. He said to the curator, "Let us not talk any more tonight. The child is over-excited."

The Sun sent a gorgeous rainbow for her to travel on.

"All right, let him rest.   But let me tell you that I have been on that island and I have walked through cactus thickets to get to a certain cave on the western side.   The cave can only be entered at low tide, and it is guarded by rough rocks.   Most amazing of all, it is lined with rock crystal and glitters above the boiling, foaming waters on its beach.   It is a high cave with two floors, and how this Navaho boy knows about it is beyond me."

"It's great stuff, this tying up fiction with facts," said the Big Man.   "Now let us leave the family to sleep for the night. They will all be happy on the floor with your rugs and skins."

CHAPTER XXIII

STORY OF THE WESTERN CLANS

HEN morning came plans were made for building Mother's loom in the patio of the museum. The curator ordered sycamore limbs to be brought, and Mother soon had the two posts firmly set in the ground. To these she tied a cross piece at top and bottom, and proceeded to make the frame for the woolen strings she wound up and down for the warp. As her rug was to be a small one she had the strings all stretched by noontime. She had brought her wool yarn with her from the desert.

A number of visitors crowded about her. They had come to see the museum exhibit of Navaho handwork. They watched Mother pass her yarn through the warp, weaving in and out, and causing patterns to grow like magic.

Father did not feel like working in silver. He was too much interested looking in the glass cases which held prehistoric articles from the Channel Islands. He and Younger Brother stayed with the Big Man, while the curator pointed out the treasures he had found in the graves on the lonely island.

Younger Brother moved from case to case, not very much interested in the things which were strange to him. Round bowls of soapstone and fish hooks of bone had no familiar meaning to him, but when he saw abalone shell ornaments and wampum beads just like those he wore on his purple velvet shirt, he said to Father, "The ancient people of this land liked shell beads, but I see no turquoise."

"I think our people have all the turquoise. They would not trade it for shells. The shells they have are reminders of the wide water, but the turquoise belongs to the desert."

"Here is a pipe shaped like the one the Sun Bearer smokes when he reaches home," said Younger Brother.

"Maybe it is his pipe," said Father.

"That cannot be so. He smokes it every night while he sits by Estsanatlehi's fire. My Uncle has told me so."

"Maybe it is an old pipe which he threw away."

"That may be. I shall ask Uncle when we return to the Waterless Mountain."

The curator was showing a stone charm to the Big Man. It was a top shaped object about three inches long. It was made of rock which looked something like soapstone and something like mutton fat jade. It was carved by hand into a design of six ridges running lengthwise. Two of the ridges were plain, one was divided into five knobs, one into four, and the other into three knobs.

The curator had found this object in a grave on the mainland and had never heard of anything like it in America. It was precious to him on account of its rarity and mystery.

When Younger Brother saw it he said simply, "My Uncle has one much like it. He uses it for healing. He presses it to the patient's legs when he has pain."

"What is it, my boy ?" asked the Big Man.

"My Uncle says it is a piece of star."

"Well," said the curator, "the migrations of the early Americans have left strange traces along the road."

The Big Man asked Younger Brother to tell what he knew of the early clans who traveled from the wide water to the desert.

The boy spoke in his soft, musical voice. "My Uncle has told me that some of our people lived here by the wide water, and when the twelve holy people of the east visited them, they listened to tales of people of their own kind who lived over the mountain and far in the desert.

"They liked the stories of what the desert people did, what they ate, and how they dressed in skins and yucca fiber. They thought they would like to join them, so they decided to ask the Turquoise Woman what she thought about it. She said, 'It is a dangerous trip, my children, and a long way to travel. I know, for I have traveled it myself. If you must go, I will give you five of my pets to protect you. Take a bear, a snake, a deer, a porcupine and a mountain lion. They will watch over you. Speak no evil in the presence of the bear and the snake, for they might do the wrong you speak of.' "

Younger Brother, standing by the case of abalone shell ornaments, pointed to them and said, "My uncle has told me that the Turquoise Woman gave a magic wand of abalone shell and one

Take a bear, a snake, a deer, a porcupine, and a mountain lion, they will watch over you.

of white shell to her children. Also my uncle said she gave them magic wands of black stone, of turquoise, and of red stone. She told the people they would need them on the way.

" 'But,' she said, 'I also will watch over you as you travel. Remember your mother always in her western home.' "

The little story teller looked up at the Big Man, and a smile of happiness spread over his face. "I have remembered her," he said. "Always I have thought of the mother of all of us, and I am glad that I left my sheep to come here to make my offering. Uncle will be happy to have the Paiute wicker jar filled with the sacred water."

"We are all glad you came," said the Big Man. "Did Uncle tell you more of the people who traveled east?"

"He has told me much, but I cannot remember all. I like to think of the pet bear watching by the camps at night, and growling at any danger."

"What did the people do with the magic wands, my boy?"

"As the people traveled, they came to a great plain where there was no water. The little children cried, for they were thirsty. The men said, 'Let us try the magic of our wands.' So the owner of the turquoise wand struck it into the ground and worked it round and round until the hole was big. Then water sprang from the hole, but it was bitter. They drank it and cooked with it, and then moved on for four days. Because there was still no water, they thrust the white shell wand into the ground. The water which came was muddy and it made the children sick.

"Many days they traveled and many days they were thirsty

and the children cried. They passed white alkaline ground, mile after mile glaring in the sun."

The Big Man said, "That must have been in the Death Valley Region."

"After forty days the travelers reached the mountain which we call Dokoslid. It is the western mountain which I climbed, Grandfather. That is the mountain where I left my prayer stick with the yellow warbler feathers."

"I know the mountain well," said the Big Man. "Always its peak is white with snow."

"The western people carried abalone shells to the mountain, Grandfather. And while they camped on its eastern side they built a stone wall which still stands. It was there the mountain lion killed a deer. The pet bear sometimes killed rabbits."

"It was a good camp, I am sure," said the Big Man.

"It is still a good camp. There is where I slept two nights and there is where I saw the Deer People at the spring."

As Younger Brother finished his story of the migration from the west, Father walked down the big room looking at the work of the prehistoric people. He was getting tired. He had seen enough; more than enough, because at the far end of the room he had come to an exhibit of very old skulls.

He said in a frightened voice, "Chindi !" and ran from the room to sit by Mother's loom. The others followed and the Big Man heard Father say to Mother, "Why do Pelicanos keep bones in their hogans ? I do not like it here. I want to go back home where the dead stay buried."

"This is a strange place," said Mother. "Some of the women

have short hair and they have no shame, for their skirts are very short.   Not one of them can spin nor weave."

The Big Man listening, laughed to reassure his desert people. He said, "The Pelicano children are very kind to Little Sister They have given her sweet yellow fruit from their trees."

"Yes," said Mother, "little children are all right, whatever the color of their skin."

CHAPTER XXIV

THE MOVIE HERO SPEAKS

URING four days the exhibition of Navaho work attracted people to the museum. The Navaho family grew more at ease, though everyone was anxious to get back home to the sheep and the sagebrush under the shadow of Waterless Mountain.

On the last night of their stay the Big Man decided to take his charges to a movie theatre to see a talking picture which had been staged in Navaho land.

The little party walked down the street of many hogans where bright lights dazzled their eyes, and many automobiles confused them.

As they entered the theatre leaving the brilliantly lighted street, they were suddenly plunged into blackness vast and terrible.

Mother tried to run back, she was so frightened. It took much persuasion on the Big Man's part to get the family into the seats which they could not see.

As they sat there in the dark, the first picture of the play was

144

flashed on the screen. Younger Brother found himself looking at a piece of the desert he had traveled over with the Pelicano boy. He saw the very place where the boy's machine had been stuck in the mud under the colored cliffs.

He was so dazed, he thought he must be dreaming. As one scene after another was reeled off before any real action began, Younger Brother accepted the new experience as he had accepted other wonders of the Pelicanos.

When a group of Navahos on their ponies were shown riding across a stretch of sand to dismount in front of a trading post, he became more interested.

He watched intently and as a close up picture of the riders was shown, he became much excited and said to the Big Man sitting next to him, "That is Cut Finger who tried to steal my pony."

The pictures reeled off too fast for the unaccustomed eyes of the boy, leaving his mind confused by sight and sound. He could not understand what was happening. There was much white man's talk, and noise of horse hoofs beating on rocks. A big Pelicano sat on a white horse which stood in the sunlight under shadowed cliffs.

Younger Brother thought the horse was a beauty. While he was busy admiring it, he was suddenly conscious that a very strange thing was happening on the screen. The picture showed a tall Navaho man, dressed with velveteen shirt, walking slowly toward the Pelicano. His soft moccasined feet made no sound as he moved across the sunlit sand at the base of the cliff.

As Younger Brother watched the figure move toward the white horse with the Pelicano he began to tremble violently.

The Big Man wondered what ailed the boy. He put his hand on his knee to comfort him.

Just then the Navaho in the picture spoke one word, "Ahalani, Greeting."

It was the voice of the beautiful young husband of Younger Brother's relative.

The trembling boy, looking at the picture was terrified beyond control. He jumped from his seat, crying, "Chindi, Chindi, ghost !"

He ran wildly toward the theatre door, stumbling in the darkness, sobbing and utterly distraught.

The Big Man and the boy's parents followed him. He ran out of the theatre onto the street, and when they stopped him he was still crying and trembling. With difficulty the Big Man managed to get the boy back to the home of the curator.

There he quieted him, while Father and Mother stood by helplessly. He told the boy more about the white man's cameras, and tried to dispel the terrible fear which had come over him.

When the boy was able to talk coherently, he said to his mother, "The husband of your relative was too beautiful. I know now. The Pelicano saw his perfect beauty. They made the picture of him and the Yays were jealous. They destroyed him in the flood. It is not well that anything be overdone. I must go back to my Uncle at the Waterless Mountain. I need to tell him what I have learned."

The Big Man said, "Yes, we must all go back. We do not belong here. There is too much noise and too much heaping of goods."

In the morning before they left the place of many hogans, Younger Brother went down to the wide water alone. He looked across its blue breadth to the blue island. He reached out his arms toward the west, and said:

"Mother of all of us, I shall not forget the trail of beauty the Sun Bearer travels to your hearth. I shall tell Uncle when I give the water to him, that you are watching your children. Now I return."

It was a happy group that waited at the railroad station to board the train. The Big Man said to Father:

"Hasteen, where did you get those sheep horns ?"

"I took them from the wall of the Pelicano's hogan. I want them for my sheep. If I burn a little piece of horn in the corral, my sheep will increase. The Pelicano let me have them."

Mother carried her loom and Sister was loaded down with presents the children had given her. Under one arm she carried a toy bureau and a teddy bear. Younger Brother had his jar of water and an abalone shell.

The Big Man said to the conductor, "We may need a baggage car."

So, laughing, they said goodbye to the kind Pelicano and left the wide water of the west.

CHAPTER XXV

THE HOUSE DEDICATION

T HOME again in the early autumn, Younger Brother felt content. Uncle had given him a purification ceremony and a sweat bath in the little mud house made for that purpose.

Stones had been heated in a fire outside the tiny hut, and had been shoveled into the sweat house. Younger Brother crawled through the small door. He had removed all his clothes and had taken a big drink of warm water.

Blankets at the doorway shut in the heat and the air grew very hot. Younger Brother felt the sweat pouring out through his skin and after a sufficient time he went outside, steaming all over. He dried himself with sand which he rubbed on his wet skin.

After that he felt fine and knew that everything Uncle was doing for him was good. He lost the memory of his fright in the Pelicanos' dark picture house where chindis talked. He remembered only the blue island and the blue water where the Turquoise Woman lived in beauty.

He was lying in the morning sunshine by his mother's camp-fire. Little Sister had just put a cedar stick on the fire under the dye pot. Mother was spinning natural brown wool which she was to weave with the yarn that she was dyeing red.

The turquoise sky behind the Waterless Mountain must have shaken bits of itself to earth, thought Younger Brother, as he watched a big flock of bluebirds flying to the overflow of the water tank for their morning drink.

"Never have I seen so many bluebirds," said the boy.

Mother looked toward the brilliant moving specks of blue and said:

"There are many and I think they have come down from the north too early. The northern people must have sent them to us."

"That means early winter weather. Uncle has told me so. He says that when the snow comes, our northern brothers are looking south."

"Your uncle knows. He is wise. I am glad we are home again with him and Elder Brother and the sheep."

"It is good," said the boy. "Elder Brother says he is building a new hogan for his family, and the house blessing will be soon."

"Yes," said Mother. "We will all go. There will be much good food to eat. There will be mutton and corn bread."

Two days later the whole family rode to the new home of Elder Brother. It was built on a little knoll surrounded by juniper and piñon trees. Orange-colored sandstone buttes rose behind the knoll. In front the rolling ground stretched away toward purple mountain ranges.

To the east Waterless Mountain stood, with its long, straight top, and steep, canyoned sides. It was a very big mountain, extending many miles in every direction.

Uncle said that on all of its sides, east, south, west, and north there was not a single spring of water.

It was such a high mountain that in the winter time, snow lay on its flat top, giving moisture to the pine and spruce forests that massed just below its crest. Its steep rocky sides gave little support to vegetation.

Younger Brother often wished he might climb its wind-carved cliffs. Once more he thought so as he sat outside the new hogan, waiting with all the relatives for Elder Brother and his wife to finish their house blessing.

Inside, Elder Brother made the fire, while his wife swept the floor with a bunch of grass. When that was done the wife handed a basket of white corn meal to her husband. He took a little of the meal and rubbed it on the south timber of the doorway as high as he could reach.

Moving in the sunwise direction, to the west and north timbers, he silently made the gift of corn meal to the house where he and his family were to live.

When this was done, he sprinkled the meal on the floor at the base of the timbers, saying in low, measured tones:

> *May it be delightful, my house.*
> *From my head to my feet*
> *May it be delightful.*
> *Where I lie may it be delightful.*

All above me may it be delightful.
All around me may it be delightful.

While Elder Brother went through this ceremony, his wife
watched and listened with quiet happiness. She saw him fling
a bit of meal into the fire he had made and she heard him say:

May my fire be delightful.

She watched him throw a bit toward the ceiling. The words
he then spoke were addressed to the sun:

Accept this gift, Oh, Bearer of the Day.
May it be delightful as I walk about my house.

Then from the open doorway Elder Brother sprinkled the
white corn meal toward the east, saying:

May this road of light ever and always lead
in peace to my home.

After that he handed the basket to his wife and she spoke
the words of blessing that Uncle had taught her. She went to
the sweet cedar fire that her husband had lit for her and said
in a low voice:

May it be delightful my fire.
May it be delightful for my children.
May all be well.
May it be delightful with my food and theirs.
May all be well.

All of my possessions, may they be made to increase.
And my flocks, may they be made to increase.

The blessing was finished. The people outside now entered the hogan and sat about the fire. The women brought in the food they had been preparing all day and set it down for the men to eat. Younger Brother ate with the others, enjoying again mutton roasted over the open fire.

He thought his sister-in-law looked very pretty in her new dress. She sat on a sheepskin, with her two babies. Little Sister was playing with the baby strapped in its cradle and both were laughing.

After the fine feast was finished, the men smoked tobacco, which they rolled in corn husks. Then everyone talked for two hours before leaving for home.

The wife of Elder Brother arranged with Uncle to come again in four nights and sing his songs of blessing. She told him she would give him two sheep for doing so.

Younger Brother decided to stay at the new hogan for a few days to visit with his sister-in-law. He told her everything that had happened on his journey to the wide water.

She thought he was a wonderful boy. They were sitting outside the hogan, facing the Waterless Mountain. She was sewing on a little dress for her baby.

She liked the story of the Deer People who had walked past Younger Brother when he camped at the western mountain. She said:

"Were you afraid when you were all alone ?"

It was a mile from the hogan to Standing Rock.

"Sometimes I was afraid but always it was of hidden things. I was never afraid of what I could see and smell and hear."

"You were just afraid of chindi. I know. They come out of nowhere. I do not like them either."

The boy looked at her and said, "They cannot hurt you if you say, 'The trail is beautiful, be still.' If you say that Estsanatlehi will drive away the bad ones. Uncle told me that long ago."

"Uncle is coming tonight to bless my hogan. I am glad of that for I want only good dreams here. I will give him two of my best sheep for singing the songs of blessing."

"That is only right. Uncle's songs are worth that much." Just then Elder Brother rode up on his pony. He did not dismount but sat in his saddle looking at Younger Brother's pinto tied to a tree.

"Your pony looks fat and lazy," he said to Younger Brother.

"My pony is not lazy."

"His legs are unused. I think he cannot run."

"He will show you that he can run," said the boy, as he untied the spotted horse and jumped into the saddle.

Before Elder Brother realized that a race was on, Younger Brother had a start of a hundred yards. The two brothers urged their ponies toward Standing Rock. They rode wildly, with their elbows out and flapping like wings.

It was a mile run from the hogan to the rock and Spotted Horse won. The brothers rode leisurely back, laughing and talking about the big feast to be given that night in the hogan.

"They say," said Elder Brother, "that there will be beef and blue corn dumplings wrapped in husks."

"They say there will be sweet watermelons too," said Younger Brother.

The brothers were not disappointed when darkness came and the company sat about the fire, eating.

Uncle started the house songs of the east and west. All the men joined in and sang in lively fashion. They sang all night so that the last song was given just as the dawn broke over Waterless Mountain.

CHAPTER XXVI

ON THE MOUNTAIN TOP

S THE company left the hogan Younger Brother and Uncle lingered in the doorway looking toward Waterless Mountain, with its long, straight top purple against the sky. The boy said, "I have never been up there. I think I should like to go."

"I have never been on top," said Uncle, "but I know there is spruce growing there. I think we should go, you and I."

The boy was very happy at the thought. For the next two days he helped Uncle get ready for the trip. They decided to take one pack animal to carry the blankets and sheepskins, food and a keg of water. Each rider had a small canteen of water tied to his saddle for Uncle said:

"We travel in a country without springs. We Navahos call it the Waterless Mountain, because on its top and on all of its sides there is not one spring; but no one knows what may be in its heart. There are six directions always, east, south, west, north, above, and below. Below is the deep heart of things."

As Uncle and Younger Brother rode up the wash, the boy kept thinking of what Uncle had said.

"Who knows what may be in its heart."

Deep, deep down under the earth were many mysteries and the source of many wonders. Uncle had told him of the Water People, who kept the rainbows in the heart of the earth, to send to the Sky People when they needed them to travel on.

As the two passed at the bottom of the cliffs on whose top was the big pool that poured its water down through the pipe, Younger Brother said to Uncle:

"Where does the water in the big pool come from ?"

"It must come from some higher place," said Uncle.

"There is no higher place in sight except the Waterless Mountain."

"That is true, but what of it, child ?"

"I was thinking about the deep heart of things. Maybe the Waterless Mountain has a pool buried in the deep below. Maybe it sends a river underground to the pool of the mesa."

Uncle looked at the boy with pride and said:

"Once you sang a new song. I knew then you were made to follow me. Now you have spoken wisdom about the beginning of things, and the water from whence we came."

"I speak only as my heart sings. Sometimes it sings till I feel pain deep down. Why should that be, Uncle ?"

"There are some truths you are yet too young to know, Little Singer. It is better that you watch your pony now as we climb the loose rocks. Soon we shall camp for the night."

After another hour's riding, the two made camp in a sandy

hollow among the rocks, where one lone juniper tree lifted its dark branches above twisted gray roots.

Uncle hung the bridles on the juniper limbs, piled the saddles at its base, and put the water keg where Younger Brother could pour water for cooking. Then he tied the three horses about a hundred feet away from the camp.

The boy gathered sagebrush and juniper bark for the fire, while Uncle lay down on the sand to smoke the cigarette he had rolled in a corn husk.

While Younger Brother spread the sheepskins on the ground, the coffee boiled on the fire and the mutton ribs sizzled. Both the travelers were hungry. They liked the cold tomatoes eaten right out of the can. They went fine with the mutton.

By the time dusk had settled on the hills around, Uncle and Younger Brother lay back on the sheepskins with their feet to the fire and talked of the wonders the boy had seen at the wide water.

"I have saved the jar of water you brought. I shall need it at the next dance of the Yays, when the white earth will be mixed with the western water to make the paint for their bodies."

"I am glad I brought it, Uncle."

The boy was watching the stars appear in the blue-black sky.

"Did you once tell me that Coyote put the lights in the sky ?"

"Yes, First Man asked him to because the moon was not there every night and it was too dark. First Man planned the big star in the north, the star that never moves, and he planned the seven stars that move around it there."

"What did he make the stars of ?" asked Younger Brother as he lay on his back watching the bright spots sparkling above.

"They were made of pieces of shining mica. First Man drew a plan on the sand, putting the mica in the places where he wanted the stars to be in the sky. Then along came Coyote and said 'I want these three red pieces for my very own.'

" 'All right,' said First Man, 'but help me throw them all up in the right place.'

"So they threw the big pieces of mica up against the dark sky and they stuck just where they wanted them to. After Coyote had placed his three red ones he was no longer interested so he just took all the mica that was left and placed it in his hands and blew on it.

"Puff, puff, he blew, and all the sparkling mica went up and stuck to the sky most anywhere. That is why we do not know the names of all the stars. They have no names because they never did have."

"It doesn't matter very much about names, Uncle, so long as there are things to think about. If my heart sings, I know it and I couldn't tell anyone the name of the song."

"That is because you are made for a real medicine man. We never name the things we sing because that would make them common."

"Is that why mothers do not speak their children's names ?"

"That is just the reason. Children are precious and mothers do not want everyone in the world knowing what name sings in the mother's heart."

"Only once, Uncle, has my mother called me by the name she gave me."

"When was that, child ?"

"That was when I was sick with heat in the head and when the Big Man came with the sweet yellow fruit.   Mother sat on the floor beside me while we were alone.   She held my hand in her cool hand and she leaned over me while my eyes were shut and she whispered, 'Hayolkai Aski, my little Dawn Boy.' I liked the name my mother made for me."

"It is a good name.   We will not speak it often because we do not want it to lose its power.   Now let us sleep, child."

Uncle wrapped the blanket close around the little dawn child of his sister, pulled his own cover close about him and turned on his side to sleep.

It must have been long after midnight when Uncle was awakened by the distant cry of a prowling beast.   He was not familiar with the sound.   It was not like the yelping of coyotes nor of foxes.   It was a terrifying yell of some big animal, which drew nearer and nearer to the camp.

Uncle sat up to listen.   He looked at Younger Brother sleeping peacefully by the little glowing campfire, totally unaware of the cry that was coming closer.

Uncle lay down again, perfectly still.   As he listened he could hear at intervals between the hoarse yelps, the occasional crunching of small branches.   He knew the night prowler was approaching.   The animal no longer cried.   Soon, Uncle saw a large, shadowy form moving about ten feet beyond Younger Brother.

Breathlessly Uncle watched and waited for the lithe figure to move on. With slow, deliberate steps and with head pointed straight forward, the big animal walked on past the camp without further cries.

Uncle knew that the Soft-footed Chief was on the scent of the horses which were tied about a hundred feet away. He rose quietly, seized a piece of juniper bark lying by the coals, dipped it in the fire and lit it, then ran quickly in the direction of the horses. He found them trembling with fear and trying to break away.

In the darkness he could not see the mountain lion but he stood by the horses and waved the firebrand. Soon, as he watched, he saw two glowing eyes shining out of the blackness. He shook the burning bark in front of the eyes until they moved away. Then he uttered a prayer ending with these words:

"Walk away in peace, Soft-footed Chief. Walk on the trail of beauty."

Then Uncle untied the animals and led them to the camp.

"Wake up," he said to Younger Brother. "It is time to make our coffee."

After throwing some sagebrush on to the fire, Uncle tied the horses to the lone juniper tree and proceeded to put the saddles on them.

"Why do we wake so early?" asked the sleepy boy.

"I will tell you when the dawn shows in the sky. Now you make the coffee. I feel the need of it."

Younger Brother made the coffee. He was puzzled. His

Uncle's hand trembled when he took the coffee cup. He said, "I am just a little cold."

Soon the gray light made things visible and Younger Brother went to gather more fuel for the fire. As he came back he stopped a few feet from where he had been sleeping and examined the sand.

"Uncle," he cried. "Some big animal passed in the night. Here are his tracks."

"Yes, my child. It was the Soft-footed Chief that passed. I spoke to him. I showed him the firebrand. He left, but he might come back."

The boy said excitedly:

"What did he look like, Uncle? Never have I seen him."

"He looked like a mighty chief, the way he walked in slowness, and his voice was more powerful than any I have heard."

"I wish that I too might have seen him."

"It is enough that I saw him. My sister's child already has the power of strong medicine. The beasts walk by him in peace."

Uncle took out his medicine bag and touched the pollen to his tongue and his head, and threw some to the sun, which was just rising in the east. He passed the pollen to Younger Brother, who repeated the ceremony. Each said in his heart the silent prayer to the day.

By the time the sun was just above the horizon, the two riders were well on their way up a narrow gully filled with slabs of bright-colored sandstone and prickly cactus plants.

Uncle said, "The Cactus People always live in a land of

mirage and bright rocks. They are a mighty people, who can cure trouble of the skin."

"I should think they could cause trouble, too," said the boy.

When the riders had nearly reached the top of the mountain, Uncle dismounted to pick some stalks of mountain tobacco, which grows only in high altitudes.

"This is for the sacred cigarettes of the Night Chant," he said. "I am glad that I have found it."

He carefully wrapped the stalks in a flour sack and tied the bundle to his saddle. Before very long the top of the mountain was reached. The riders jumped from their horses and sat down to enjoy a quiet smoke.

Looking back to the country they had left the day before, it was hard to realize that they had crossed deep canyons and climbed steep hills. The land lay flattened out in the distance.

Uncle waved his hand in an eloquent gesture from east to south, from west to north. Then pointing, he said:

"There is where my mother's people made war on the Apaches. There is where my father's people took the scalps of the Utes. There is where we captured the Mexicans, and there is the canyon where Kit Carson made us take the Long Walk. Some of us hid in the mountains where no Pelicanos have ever been."

"Did any of us hide here ?" asked Younger Brother.

"That I cannot say. If there was no water here, it would not be a good hiding place. Let us walk to the north slope and see if any snow is left under the trees."

They found some snow and melted a little over a fire so that the horses could have a good drink. They also filled their keg and canteens with melted snow.

While doing this Younger Brother noticed a queer little rock sticking out of the pine needles. He picked it up and found fossil sea shells imbedded in it.

"Look," he cried. "The wide water has been here at some time."

"Yes, it must have been here. Of that time I know nothing, but there are bones of ancient monsters in all our land."

Younger Brother put the shells in his pocket. He would give them to Sister when he reached home.

Uncle cut some spruce boughs and tied them on the pack horse. The little cavalcade started down the mountain. Uncle said:

"I am glad we came because I need the mountain tobacco and the spruce. But we will go quickly home and not disturb the Soft-footed Chief tonight. I have seen how far spreads the land of my mothers and grandmothers and I feel light and happy within."

The travelers reached home after dark, very glad to rest safely in Mother's warm hogan.

CHAPTER XXVII

THE PACK RAT'S NEST

NCE more winter stood back to back with summer and the frost had made its presence felt. The old men told stories as they sat around the hogan fires. Every family was at home, for no nuts were on the piñon trees, and there was no need to go to the mountains. It was a bad winter for everyone. The traders could not pay cash for rugs and skins. They could not afford to loan money on the jewelry. Already too much turquoise and coral and silver hung unredeemed high above the counter.

Many families were forced to go without sugar and coffee. The Big Man did all he could to keep the people from going hungry.

Uncle said, "We have our sheep. We will not go hungry and we can keep warm in our hogans. My father has told me that when our people came back from exile when I was a little boy, they were so hungry that they ate roots and seeds of grass. Many times we have hungered in the past, but that has made us strong. Shall we be soft now ?"

"Tell us more of the exile, Uncle," said Younger Brother. "I like to hear about the Long Walk."

The family, including Elder Brother and his wife, were sitting about the fire. Father had just entered with an armful of wood. There were flakes of snow on his fur hat and on his blanket. He said:

"The northern brothers are facing us many times this winter."

"Yes," said Uncle. "The springs should flow with plenty after this. I shall feel like singing of the corn. My father once told me something that my heart remembers."

All were quiet and attentive for they knew that Uncle was about to tell a story. He began:

"My mother's brother was a singer of the Night Chant. He lived with his family near Standing Rock. He owned a set of the deerskin masks used by the Yays in the Night Chant.

"When the order came from Washington to send the Navahos to Fort Sumner, because some of them had been stealing Mexican horses, my uncle was much worried about the masks.

"They were very sacred to his people and he felt the responsibility of keeping them. He decided that he must hide them safely until the return of the people, so he carefully packed them in four big pottery jars, and hid the jars somewhere in the cliffs."

Younger Brother's eyes gleamed brighter and brighter as he listened to the story of the hidden masks. He was suddenly fired with ambition to find them.

Uncle continued his story as it had been told him by his father:

"After my uncle hid the masks, he walked with the other men toward the east, away from the home of their mothers. For four years they were kept there, where the white soldiers gave them food, but they were not happy because they were always thinking of the old home of their mothers. My uncle sickened and before he died he told my father how he had hidden the masks, but my father could never find them. In some cliff in this neighborhood I know they are living in beauty."

Younger Brother spoke excitedly:

"I will find them for they belong to us. We need them for our people. If we sang the songs of plenty with the old masks, the Hunger People would leave."

Uncle looked fondly at the boy. He had faith that he would find them, for he was a chosen medicine man. Had not the Soft-footed Chief walked past him in beauty? Had he not talked with the Turquoise Woman in her western home and brought back a shell from the wide water ?

Uncle went on with his story:

"I have heard from my father that the medicine man, who was my mother's brother, owned twenty masks of unwounded buckskin. I have heard that my mother's brother put four masks in one jar, four masks in another jar, six in a third jar, and the other six, which were masks of female deities, in the fourth jar. My mother's brother told my father when they went on the Long Walk that he had hidden the four jars in the cliffs near his home. His home was not far from here. I think it was near where the new water tank stands today."

Everyone listened in silence. Younger Brother kept very quiet but he was thinking hard. Finally he said:

"The jars must be in a big cave, Uncle."

"I know of no big cave, child, but the footsteps of the ancients are carved in the red rocks that rise above the new water tank."

Younger Brother looked very wise as he answered:

"I too have seen the footsteps of the ancients. I saw them when I climbed the red rocks to find the water."

"Did you see any big caves ?" asked Father.

"No, I saw only fallen rocks, which cut my moccasins. It was hard to climb to the pool. I did it with my hands and feet and only I have climbed that way."

Father said:

"If there are footholds of the ancient people in the red rocks, they led to the pool. Always there have been people near water. The homes of the ancients are hidden by fallen rocks and I think we should not disturb them. It is not good to dig among the ruins."

While they talked, Younger Brother lay on his sheepskin by the fire. He was thinking, trying to remember something. His sister-in-law sat next to him. Her two babies were asleep in the corner of the room.

Younger Brother noticed that she still wore the deer hoof tied to the fringe of her belt. Always when she was near him, Younger Brother felt happy. She reminded him of the days when he first learned the songs of his people. He recalled his treasure cave and the little silver button that had fallen from her moccasin when she raced to the dawn.

He still kept the silver button and the red stone and the petri-fied wood. They were in the pottery bowl in Uncle's hogan. Thinking of his petrified wood of the four colors made him think of the time the Pack Rat had changed the colors of the north and east in his treasure cave.

He remembered how he had watched the Pack Rat scamper out of the cave and run in a certain direction. Suddenly he remembered something else, something he had hardly noticed at the time. The Pack Rat had disappeared under a big rock surrounded by a pile of small rocks. The big rock was in a little canyon above the treasure cave.

The Pack Rat had piled twigs on top of the loose rocks around the entrance to his cave. Some of the twigs were dif-ferent in color and texture from the others. Younger Brother had noticed that, but had not thought much about it, but now he had one of his sudden revelations. Those twigs had come from the inside of the Pack Rat's home. They were twigs cut by men long ago. They were not like the twigs that grew around the outside of the pack rats' home. Turning to his brother's wife, Younger Brother whispered:

"I know where the four jars must be."

"Where must they be, Little Singer ?"

"They must be in the home of the Pack Rat under the big rock," said the boy.

The young woman looked at him with the far-away look in her eyes and said:

"I have heard Uncle tell the story of four jars in the home of the Pack Rat. They must be there."

Younger Brother said nothing more about the matter that night. He wanted to investigate for himself and by himself. Early in the morning he went alone to the home of the Pack Rat. He examined the twigs and rubbish heaped about the entrance. To his amazement he found a piece of reed the length of three finger widths. The reed was painted black.

Younger Brother recognized it as part of a prayer stick used in the Night Chant. He ran home full of excitement. He must tell Uncle immediately.

Uncle said:

"The Pack Rat always guides you, Little Singer. We must clear away the rocks that cover his home."

"I think we shall need much help, Uncle. Maybe the Big Man would tell us what to do. He understands the power of the Pack Rat, even as we do, Uncle."

"Very well, we will tell him. We can ride to the trading post today. I need more tobacco."

CHAPTER XXVIII

FOUR POTS IN A CAVE

T THE trading post, Uncle and Younger Brother found a number of Navahos warming their hands near the big stove in the middle of the store. They were talking about what some Indian had done. Younger Brother heard the name "Cut Finger." He listened.

"He has burned a trading post up in the mountains."

"Is that so? What will the Pelicanos do to him for that?"

"They will have to find him before they can do anything. He is hiding."

"Always that man is crazy. He makes trouble for the Navahos."

"They say he was hungry. They say he saw the silver pawn hanging in the store."

"Did he steal the pawn?"

"Yes, he broke the window and stole the pawn and then set fire to the store."

"Where was the trader?"

"He was at the agency. It was Sunday and he left the post alone."

"That Cut Finger is bad. He should be shut up. He drinks too much mule whiskey."

Younger Brother listened. He remembered how Cut Finger had tried to get away with his pony. He remembered his squint eyes and the cruel mouth. He hoped the Navaho policeman would soon catch him.

Uncle also was warming his hands over the stove. His brown fur hat was pulled down over his ears and his Pendleton blanket hung loose from his shoulders. He said to the group of Navahos about him:

"Where is the place where Cut Finger burned the post ?"

"It is near the water of Red Canyon far to the west of here. There are many box canyons to hide in."

"Does the policeman ride to find Cut Finger ?"

"He is getting ready now. He is in the little room with the Big Man."

Uncle, followed by Younger Brother, entered the little room at the back of the store. The Big Man sat at his desk with his typewriter before him. He greeted his good friends kindly and introduced the Navaho policeman, who was a stranger to Uncle.

They discussed the burning of the store and Younger Brother listened attentively. He heard the Big Man say:

"That trader is a good friend of mine. I am sorry for him. He will need help. Cut Finger must be found. No doubt he is hiding in one of those washes."

"I think I know where he hides," spoke up Younger Brother.

The policeman looked at the boy and laughed.

"Where does he hide, little fox ?"

"When he stole my pony, he rode toward the north from the wash, which runs east of the big rock where two junipers grow close together. He rode north toward a hill of blue clay. I think he hides there."

The Big Man said to the policeman, "Do you know where that blue hill is ?"

"Yes, I have seen it."

"Well, take your men and ride there now. I have had the food packed and the canteens filled with water. It is a long ride."

"I will go there. I have to start hunting in some place."

After he left, Uncle told the Big Man about the Pack Rat's nest, and about the loose rocks, and how he wanted to find the jars. He said:

"Grandfather, we need help to move the rocks. Can you ask the Pelicano who fixes the water holes for us, to do this work ?"

"It is not what he is paid to do, but I can ask him. I should like to see for myself where the Pack Rat lives."

"We must not disturb the Pack Rat, Grandfather. We will have to be kind to him for he knows about the east and north."

"All right, we will watch out. I think it can be done soon, while the policeman is looking for Cut Finger."

"And Grandfather, when we find the masks of my mother's uncle, I will sing the Night Chant. Now I need tobacco."

The Big Man passed a cigar to Uncle and told the store clerk to furnish him with plug. Uncle and Younger Brother rode home.

In two days the Big Man arrived in his car with the water developer, who looked at the pile of rubble that had lodged around the big rock. He traced it back up the side of the cliff, and decided that there must have been a landslide that could have covered the opening of a cave.

The Pack Rat's nest evidently had its outlet at the lower end of the slide. In that case the loose rocks could be removed without disturbing the nest. Uncle insisted that the Pack Rat People must not be troubled, because they had always been very wise in their teachings. He had never forgotten about their changing the colors of the north and east.

He was sure they were still trying to teach Younger Brother something about the east, for they had placed the little black prayer stick on top of their nest for the boy to find.

Uncle sat by the entrance to the nest, watching the men shoveling under the direction of the Pelicano. Younger Brother was much excited. He watched every shovelful of dirt. He was sure the workers would find a cave.

About noon of the second day, enough rubble had been cleared away to show that the big rock did run back, making a roof over an opening under it. As soon as the hole was big enough to admit a man, the water developer and the trader crawled in. The rest of the party waited outside.

The two explorers found that they must jump down to the floor of the cave. They were provided with candles and matches. They had ample room to walk comfortably. They noticed shelving rocks inside and signs of old walls built up as partitions.

"Conklin," said the Big Man, "this looks like one of the earliest types of building. The old people used the natural rock for floor and roof and built these partitions to make separate little rooms."

"It's surely interesting, to say the least."

Just as he spoke, something in the blackness behind them rattled a little.

"What's that ?" asked the trader.

"It doesn't sound like a rattlesnake," said his companion. 'It's more like little feet scurrying."

Just then two very bright, round eyes gleamed in the candle light. Conklin said, "Why, it's the Pack Rat. I guess he occupies the whole suite. Watch where he goes."

They watched the little fellow clamber up to a ledge above their heads. They climbed up high enough to look into the recess, and by the light of their candles they could see the form of a big, dark jar.

"We will not touch a thing, Conklin. Uncle must take care of this treasure."

Outside the cave, Uncle and Younger Brother waited patiently to hear what had happened. When the two explorers climbed out into the sunshine, the Big Man said to Uncle:

"The jars are there. It is for you to take care of them. We will go now so that you can greet the masks of the Yays."

When Uncle and Younger Brother were alone they sat

The Pack Rat peered down from the ledge.

quietly for a while. They feared to enter the cave. Uncle said there should be a ceremony or a blessing to make it right for them to enter. So he said a prayer from the Night Chant and sprinkled pollen before him as he and Younger Brother climbed into the opening.

"It is larger than I thought," said Uncle, "and I do not like to enter the home of the Ancients."

"There have been Bat People here, Uncle, since the Ancients left."

"It is a place such as I never before have entered. Here are small corn-cobs heaped in a corner."

"And here is a grinding stone, Uncle."

"Touch nothing, my child, that belongs to the Ancients. We must find the jars, for they belong to us."

"I do not know where to find them, Uncle."

"I think we should walk toward the east."

"Yes, Uncle, let us walk toward the east."

They groped their way in the semi-darkness until they reached the ledge where the jars were stored.

"We have come to the east wall. We can go no further," said Uncle.

"What is the noise I hear ?"

"It sounds like the noise of little feet. I think it is the Pack Rat."

Looking up in the direction of the sound, Younger Brother saw the little bushy-tailed rat peering down on him from the ledge above his head. The little fellow sat quietly and un-afraid as if he knew the two seekers would do him no harm.

"I think we must climb up the ledge, Uncle."

"Yes, we must follow the Pack Rat, for he is our guide."

Climbing up the rocks to where the little animal sat, Uncle looked about him and saw the big dark jar. On the floor in front of the jar he noticed a shining piece of black stone. He said to Younger Brother:

"Look, here is the black stone of the east, placed by the first jar."

The boy was very much impressed when he looked at the stone. He said, "That is the little piece of petrified wood I used to keep in my treasure cave. The Pack Rat has had it for many years."

"Do not touch it, child. Leave it for the Pack Rat. He guided us to the jars that hold the masks of my mother's brother."

When Uncle removed the first jar, he found the other three behind it. They were all carefully covered with flat rocks. Uncle took all of the jars out into the sunshine. He looked inside to make sure that the masks were there, then packed the jars carefully in his wagon, and drove to his hogan, where he could examine the masks at his leisure.

News of the finding of the old masks spread for miles around. Such an important event inspired all the medicine men. They were glad that Uncle was to sing the Night Chant, using the masks of his mother's brother.

All the young men singers practiced their songs for the ninth night. Hasteen Sani chose to be the patient. It would be the fourth time in his life that he had had the ceremony.

After that he would be allowed to give the sing himself. He, too, was a student of Uncle's.

The time was set for the building of the medicine lodge and the strong clan brothers of Hasteen Sani went to the mountains to cut the pine logs and to haul firewood for all the little campfires.

Younger Brother was to assist Uncle and besides he was to be initiated for the second time. He rode with other young men to gather the sacred spruce boughs. He remembered his first trip to the forests when he was a little boy. He remembered how he had hoped to be a medicine man, and had wished to learn the old songs of his people.

With a feeling of contentment he packed the spruce boughs on his pony and rode down the mountain trail in the late afternoon sunshine. The little pinto carefully picked his way over the loose stones of the steep trail.

Younger Brother sang as he rode, lifting his face to the golden sky, where a flock of yellow warblers flung their own songs of gladness to the Bearer of the Day.

CHAPTER XXIX

COME ON THE TRAIL OF SONG

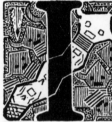N THE meantime the Navaho policeman and his posse had found Cut Finger and arrested him. He did have a hogan hidden near the blue clay hill. In a hole dug in the dirt floor he had concealed the stolen pawn. The police found not only the jewelry stolen from the burned trading post but also two fine saddle blankets and an old silver bridle set with turquoises.

Cut Finger looked uglier than ever because he was in a stupor. He was almost unconscious from too much mule whiskey. That was why it had been so easy to capture him.

The policeman put handcuffs on him and told two men to guard him while he packed the stolen articles in gunny sacks.

Silver disk belts, turquoise beads, shell and coral necklaces, earrings and bracelets had been dumped in the hole in the floor and covered with sheepskins.

The policeman recognized some of the pieces, which had been pawned by his own family. When all the jewelry had been taken out of the hole, he made another find. Underneath an old goat skin and a saddle were two big bottles of the bad whiskey.

"It is plain to see why you steal, Cut Finger. It's no use for you to say you saved the pawn of our people when you happened past the burning trading post."

"But that is what happened," insisted the drunken thief. "I saw the trader lock his door and ride away. I looked in the window and I saw that the fire in the stove had spread to the floor and burned some paper there. I broke the window to get in to put out the fire, but it was burning too fast. I saw all the silver belts of our people and I took them to save them."

"That would be a good story from a good man," said the policeman. "From you it is not good. Where do you get this whiskey?"

"My friends at the railroad give it to me."

"Well, Cut Finger, we will all go to the agency and you can tell your story to the Pelicanos. We will take the pawn and the whiskey with us."

It was not easy keeping Cut Finger with them. He tried to run away on his pony, but the policeman lassoed him with a rope. They finally delivered him and his stolen goods to the care of the agent.

The pawn was returned to the trader whose store was burned. Because the loss of his post and home had made him poor, the Big Man, who was his sympathetic friend, paid him what the Indians owed on the jewelry. In that way the trader was helped and many Indians had their precious silver and turquoise back, redeemed for them by the Big Man.

That made them happy as they wanted to wear the jewelry to the sing that Uncle was to give. Everybody being poor on account of the bad season, there were not so many yards of calico and velveteen bought as was usual in the time of a sing.

However, all were kept busy, planning and working for the great ceremony. It was to be held near Mother's hogan, but far enough back so that no road passed it.

The medicine lodge was built and a roadway about thirty feet wide extended eastward three hundred feet. On this level ground the dances of the ninth night would be held.

The lodge was left alone for one day before Uncle arrived. He came in the evening, blessed the lodge inside, and started the ceremonies.

For four days everyone in the lodge was busy making sacred cigarettes and round rings of twigs with feathers attached. Uncle sang songs, the patient was given sweat baths out of doors, and something happened every minute. Younger Brother stayed close to Uncle, watching everything that was done and helping where he could.

On the fourth night about nine o'clock, Uncle's assistant laid blankets on the ground, northwest of the fire. On top of the blankets they spread a buffalo robe. On top of that, many yards of new calico were laid, and on top of all, a fine white buckskin.

Then the twenty precious masks, which Uncle's uncle had saved in the jars, were placed in two rows on the buckskin. They were face up, with their tops toward the fire. By the side of the masks, the assistants placed rattles, a basket of plumes, fox skins, and medicine bags.

The patient, Hasteen Sani, sprinkled pollen on the masks, while he prayed in a low voice.   After that was done, everyone sat back in his place.   There were about fifteen friends of Hasteen Sani in the medicine lodge.   All were very quiet, sitting around the edge of the sacred lodge, with its fire in the middle, and Uncle sitting on the west.

Younger Brother was worshipful and intense.   This was one of the most important moments in his life — sitting next to Uncle and the twenty buckskin masks.

While everyone waited expectantly in the firelight, a crier outside the medicine lodge called:

"Bike hatali haku — Come on the trail of song."

Younger Brother saw the curtain at the doorway thrown aside and he saw a woman enter with two bowls in her hand. She was followed by many more women, all bearing old pottery bowls or modern dishes filled with food.

The women, dressed in brilliantly colored plush waists and full calico skirts, with their black, shining hair knotted at the back of their heads, walked in single file, slowly around the fire.   They walked sunwise and the leader went as far as the door on its northern side.   There were enough women to form a circle around the fire, leaving the eastern side open.

When the circle had been formed, the leader of the procession put one bowl of food down on the floor in the north.   Then the last woman put her two bowls down in the south and then the leader placed her second dish by the side of the first one.

After these four dishes had been placed, the other women put theirs down in a circle around the fire, then they sat down with the rest of the company.

The food in the bowls was prepared after an ancient recipe. There was corn meal mush made without the usual cedar ashes, and there were bee-weed greens, and greens of another plant, and there was thin corn wafer bread.

The circle of dishes stood alone while the next part of the ceremony was held. This was most important because it honored the masks.

A girl and a boy, about ten years old, who had come in with the food bearers, now dipped wands of turkey plumes into the basket of sacred water and sprinkled the masks while Uncle and other medicine men sang.

Younger Brother watched every motion of the two children. He saw the litle boy pour water from a wicker jar into a gourd. He saw the little girl put four handfuls of corn meal into an earthen bowl. He watched the boy pour the water on the meal while the girl stirred it. Everyone kept very still. The masks were to be fed.

The boy put a little of the corn meal mush on the mouth of every mask and tasted some himself four times. The little girl also tasted and so did Hasteen Sani and Uncle, Younger Brother, and everyone else in the lodge.

It was a love feast, a communion, promising new life to the tribe. Younger Brother, who knew so well the legends of his people, felt the power and the peace that comes through fellowship with men and gods.

He liked to think how long the masks had lived in beauty in the cliff where the little Pack Rat had guarded them.

Younger Brother was happy and content as he listened to the songs, which lasted throughout the night.

CHAPTER XXX

THE SAND PAINTING OF THE WHIRLING LOGS

N THE morning of the sixth day, the first sand painting was made. Uncle sat in his place on the west, directing twelve young men, who poured the colored sand. All day an old man ground sandstone on a metate, for the young men to use.

He ground red, yellow and white from rocks gathered from the cliffs of the Waterless Mountain. He ground charcoal for black and mixed black and white for blue.

The first painting that the young men made illustrated the story of the Whirling Logs. It was a most beautiful painting, with the two logs crossed and bearing on each arm two holy people. Corn plants of the four sacred colors spread from the center of the design. A rainbow of red and blue outlined with white surrounded the whole picture.

Uncle had told Younger Brother the story of this painting, many times in the past. It was about a young man who lived in the early days of the Navahos. He must have been very much like Younger Brother because he was always thinking of beautiful, strange things that no one else thought about. He had heard a story of the crossed logs, which whirled around on the surface of a bottomless lake.

He wanted to visit that lake, so he hollowed out a log for a boat. There were rock crystals for windows in the sides of the log. The opening was plugged with a cloud to keep out the water as the log floated down the river.

On the way down the river the young man had many adventures. He met all the water people, like the otter, the beaver, the fish, and the water coyote. He also met a big frog and thought he was the ugliest creature he had ever seen.

The fat frog sat on a bank smoking a pipe. He drew the smoke in through his mouth and sent it out through the warts that covered his body.

"What an ugly frog," thought the young man. "How big are his eyes ! How rough is his skin ! How swollen is his throat ! How thin are his legs ! How strange he looks with the smoke coming out of his warts !"

The young man only thought these things. He did not speak them but the frog knew, by the disgusted look on his face, what he was thinking. The frog said, "Yes, I am ugly. All that you think is true." Then he went on smoking and the warts puffed out the smoke and the big eyes bulged more than ever.

The traveler had many adventures on his way to the lake When he reached there, he thought he had never seen so beautiful a place. The lake was sunk in a bowl of rocks. It was a deep, dark blue lake and the craggy rocks encircling it were all the colors of twilight. On the edge of the water, colored sand sparkled in the light, which seemed to shine from the rocks themselves.

Little streams of water ran down among the rocks. They were bordered with plants such as the young man had never seen. While he looked at the flowers and stooped to pick up the colored sand with its tiny pebbles of red and blue and green, he heard the sound of people singing.

The song came from the water. Looking out across the lake he saw the cross of logs moving toward him. On every arm of the cross sat two holy people, and they sang, "He comes for my sake. From the east he looks at me. The rain brings pollen to the tassels."

The singers were glad to see the young man and they asked him to ride around the lake with them. After that, two little children, a boy and a girl, ran on the colored sands to greet the singers as they landed. The boy carried a turquoise bowl partly filled with white corn meal. The girl had a white shell bowl of yellow corn meal.

Soon they were busy gathering frost crystals from the plants. They mixed the frost with the meal and the holy people told the young man that when he returned to his people, he must teach them how to prepare the frost crystal medicine for fever.

They also taught him how to make the sand painting of the whirling logs and ever since that time, it has been the first painting made in the Night Chant.

In Uncle's medicine lodge near the Waterless Mountain Younger Brother helped the young men draw with the colored sands on the floor. They commenced in the center of the design, working on their knees, and smoothing the foundation sand with a stick, as they moved outward. The completed design was to be fifteen feet in diameter.

It would have the crossed logs in black, with two Yays sitting on the end of each arm of the cross. Other Yays would stand at the four quarters to guide the logs. The corn plants were to branch out from the center.

Working with the soft colors and seeing the clouds and plants take form as he poured the sand, Younger Brother thought there was no fun in the world equal to this.

It was hard work, too, leaning over the drawing for hours, and once he showed a little weariness. Uncle's eagle eyes detected the fact and he said quite severely:

"He who creates beauty never tires."

When the painting was finished and surrounded by the blue and red arch of the protecting rainbow goddess, everyone felt happy and hungry.

The mothers brought kettles of steaming mutton stew into the lodge and the workers relaxed and ate with relish. Everyone dipped his fingers into the big pot to draw out his piece of meat. During the dinner hour, the men all talked and laughed and had a good time, before the ceremony of healing commenced.

For three days, paintings were made, songs were sung, and there was no time to grow lazy. The old masks were repainted and dressed with spruce collars. They were all ready for the dancers to wear on the ninth night.

Every now and then a clattering wagon, drawn by horses with their winter coats on, would stop, and camps would be made on both sides of the roadway leading east from the lodge. The brightly-colored blankets hooding the smiling faces of the women, the happy children packed in the back of the wagon with hay for the horses, and sheepskins and pots and pans for the camp, added to the excitement of the festival.

From far and near, bands of horsemen rode through the crisp winter air. Sometimes a couple of young men would leave the group and race wildly down a canyon to the cry of "Yego, yego" from the other riders.

The people rode past Standing Rock, rising like a towering island from a sea of sagebrush. They passed the hole in the mountain made by the mighty Children of the Sun when they shot their bolts of lightning.

Hundreds came, on horseback and in wagons, and in old Fords that hardly ever hit on all four cylinders. Temporary corrals were made for a few sheep that were brought along for the feast. Everyone used the water from the tank and there was enough for all.

Wagons, saddles, blankets and people made a barricade on each side of the dancing space which led from the lodge to a green bough room where the performers were to dress.

Everything was in readiness for the all-night dance of the Yays.

CHAPTER XXXI

THE DANCE OF THE YAYS

HE NIGHT was cold and frosty, and the little campfires were most welcome. Particularly welcome was the hot coffee and tea kept ready all the time for anyone that wished it.

In the silence of the chilly night, everyone waited for the Yays to leave the green bough shelter. Finally they appeared, preceded by Uncle, who wore a handsome red blanket, with a mountain lion skin draped over his shoulders.

The white-masked god followed him. Uncle walked slowly, uttering a benediction and scattering corn meal on the ground before the four masked dancers as they moved quietly forward, shaking their gourd rattles.

They sang so softly as they moved toward the west that the audience could hardly hear them. Stealthily they entered the dance ground between the little fires, while Hasteen Sani, the patient, appeared from the lodge.

He was wearing a splendid blanket of red and orange and green. In his hands he carried a basket of meal to be blessed

189

by Uncle, while the dancers moved their feet in continuous rhythm.

While all the thousand spectators sat silently watching and the thin smoke of the cedar fires rose toward the stars, Uncle spoke softly, line by line, the ancient prayer of his people.

> *You who dwell in the House of Dawn*
> *And evening twilight,*
> *You who dwell in the House of Cloud*
> *And darkening mist;*
> *The house of rain*
> *Strong as man;*
> *The house of rain*
> *Soft as woman;*
> *You who dwell in the House of Pollen*
> *And of grasshoppers,*
> *Whose door is made of the dark mist,*
> *Whose trail is the rainbow,*
> *Where zigzag lightning*
> *Stands high above,*
> *Where virile rain*
> *Stands high above,*
> *You who dwell there, come to us.*

Absolute silence hovered over the thousand Navahos gathered to hear the holy words of their fathers. The dancers kept up the hypnotic rhythm of their feet and swaying heads, through-

ut the long prayer that ended with a plea for the happiness of
he tribe.

Hasteen Sani, standing solemnly in the firelight, spoke the
ast words:

> *In beauty I walk.*
> *With beauty before me,*
> *Behind me, above me*
> *And all around.*
> *It is finished in beauty.*
> *It is finished in beauty.*
> *It is finished in beauty.*
> *It is finished in beauty.*

When the prayer was finished, the four Yays started their
dance for growing things. One dancer represented corn, one
was vegetation, one was soft grain, and the fourth was pollen.

It was a song of growing things and the Yays bent to the
ground, singing:

> *The corn comes up,*
> *The rain descends.*

All night the little fires were kept burning. At regular intervals, different groups of masked singers entered the dance
ground to sing and dance in the ancient custom of their people.

When dawn came with its bluebird song, everyone stirred
himself to listen. The Navaho voices, in weird, falsetto tones,
greeted the morning with the words:

He sings in gladness,
Bluebird sings in gladness,
As daylight comes,
As morning comes.

After the song of dawn, all the Indians packed their goods in covered wagons, Fords and saddle bags and started for home, remembering in their hearts the words of Uncle:

May they all reach home in peace.

Younger Brother had enjoyed the whole ceremony and had been so impressed with the idea of growing things that he decided to plant a garden when the right time came. He went to the trading post to tell the Big Man about it.

"Grandfather, I need some seeds."

"What kind of seeds do you need ?"

"The kind the Yays sang about in the farming songs."

"Tell me what they sang, child. What were the songs about ?"

"They were about that young man who floated down the river to the lake. He had a pet turkey."

"What did the turkey do ?"

"The turkey followed the young man and when they came to a good place for a farm, the young man sang the first farm song. He sang, *I wish I had some seed.*

"The turkey listened to that song and then he gobbled and shook white corn seed out of his wings. Then he shook all the colored corn seeds, and beans, and muskmelon seeds, and then he shook out tobacco seeds. He was a good pet."

"He sounds like a good pet," said the Big Man. "What else did he do?"

"He was a very good pet," repeated Younger Brother. "When night came and the young man lay down on the ground to sleep, he was cold. He spoke to the turkey roosting in the cedar tree above him. He said, 'My pet, I am cold.'

"Soon after, he fell asleep and while he slept, the turkey jumped down from the tree and covered the young man with his right wing. He slept soundly all night and when he awoke in the morning, the turkey wing was over him and he was all warm."

Younger Brother continued, "I wish I had a pet like that, but I have none, so I ask you for beans and muskmelon seeds, and watermelon seeds. I would like the kind that grows big and fast."

The Big Man smiled and said:

"I will send for them and when they come, you must plant them in the right season."

"I will do it, Grandfather. That will be when the Planting Stars are two fingers above the western horizon, when the sun has set."

CHAPTER XXXII

THE SONG IN THEIR HEARTS

GAIN the month of Short Corn powdered the fields with tender green. The rainbows danced among the clouds and the voice of the thunder was heard in the land. The Planting Stars in the western sky had given notice to the People of the Earth that the soil was ready to nurse the little seeds.

Uncle said, "The Planting Stars bury themselves below the edge of the earth and not until the harvest month do they come again in the eastern sky."

Younger Brother felt the need of digging in the soil. Ever since the Yays sang the farming songs of the Night Chant, he had been thinking of growing things.

He had a fine piece of ground all ready for the seeds, which the Big Man had ordered. It was not a very large piece of ground because it had to be fenced to keep out the sheep. That was the hardest part of the job—the digging of the post holes.

He decided to make his garden just like the one in the story where the pet turkey furnished the seeds, so he cut two planting sticks, one of greasewood and one of another shrub.

When the seeds came to the Big Man, he drove out to watch Younger Brother plant them. The boy was very busy with the colored corn he had obtained from Uncle.

He dug four holes on the east side of his enclosure and dropped into each hole a grain of white corn. With his greasewood stick he dug four holes on the south side and planted the blue corn. He planted yellow in the west and in the north he put variegated corn. All the time while he planted, he sang a farm song.

"Now my corn is planted, Grandfather, and when it grows high, I will come in the night to pick off leaves for Uncle to use in his medicine. Uncle told me I must pick it while the lightning flashes on it."

"Uncle knows. You do what he says."

After the corn was planted, holes were dug for the squash, the muskmelon, beans and watermelons.

"Now," said the boy, "the little seeds will learn to grow. When my melons are ripe I shall give some to you to pay for the seed."

"That is the right thing to do, child. All your people should plant gardens and then there would be food for all."

"We did have gardens once, Grandfather, and we had many peach trees in Canyon de Chelly. When we were exiled, Kit Carson killed all the peach trees in the canyons. Why did he do that, Grandfather?"

The Big Man looked very sad and answered:

"I do not know why he did it, but there are more peach trees growing there now."

"Yes, that is where we go to trade our mutton for dried peaches. We go there and to the Hopis on their mesas. We like dried peaches cooked in the winter time."

"They are good food. The White Strangers brought them to this country with the sheep and the horses. Now, my boy, when your garden grows, keep it well weeded."

Keeping the garden weeded was quite a lot of work, for every kind of seed wanted to sprout in the soft, sandy loam.

One morning while Younger Brother hoed the soil around his beans and melons, he noticed his brother's wife herding her sheep on the hill above his garden. He walked up to talk with her.

She was sitting on the ground under the piñon tree. The sheep grazed lazily among the rocks. The blue sky shone through the lacery of pine needles, looking for all the world like the turquoise necklace that brightened the dark green blouse of the young woman.

From the top of a piñon tree, the metallic notes of a sure-throated robin filled the air with joyful sounds.

Younger Brother lay on the ground with his hands clasped behind his head. His gaze wandered to the treetop where the robin sat, flinging staccato notes of joy to the whole world.

"That is good singing," said the boy. "I wonder why a robin sings like all robins, why the bluebird sings like all bluebirds, and why the yellow warblers sing like all their people."

Their gaze on the treetop where the robin flung notes of joy to the world.

"I wonder," said his sister-in-law, "why they sing at all. Yellow Beak the eagle does not sing."

The boy looked at his brother's wife. Her face was lifted toward the treetop, for she, too, watched the robin. The curve of her slender neck, encircled by turquoise mosaic, was accentuated by the mass of dark, shining hair coiled low at the back of her head.

"Do you ever sing?" the boy asked.

"Sometimes when I weave and my baby sleeps, I sing a little, but I cannot sing as the robin sings, nor as the Yays did in the Night Chant, when they sang about the soft child rain which brings the corn."

Younger Brother noticed the far-away look of longing in her eyes. He said:

"They did sing well in the Night Chant."

"They sang as our people have always sung. It was good."

"They can sing in no other way," said Younger Brother. "The robin can sing no other way. We must sing as our people have sung. I think that Yellow Beak may sing in the way of his people but you and I cannot hear him."

The boy sat up and waved his arm toward some lambs that were coming too near. He continued:

"When the Child of the Sun made the eagle out of one of the young harpies, he swung the ugly, feathered monster into the sky, and it flew away calling, 'Suk, suk, suk, suk.' It turned into a splendid eagle with strong wings, but it had no sweet song like the little birds, but I think it sings a song in its heart, which no one can hear."

"Do you think that, Little Singer ?"

"I know it. When Yellow Beak sent the feather to me, he flew into the sky keeping time to some song. His wings beat the air and the feather that fell at my feet moved down to earth to the same song."

"Why do the little birds have songs that we can hear ?"

"Because they always have had them since the Bat Woman carried feathers in her basket."

"I do not know about the Bat Woman and the feathers. Did she make the little birds ?"

"That is a long story for winter time," said the boy. "I can only tell you that the Bat Woman carried feathers of the old harpies in her burden basket, and when she walked through a field thick with wild sunflowers, little birds flew out of her basket, singing, and perched on the sunflowers. That is all I can tell you now for the snakes and the thunder might hear."

The wife of Elder Brother looked at the boy with a question burning in her dark eyes.

"Tell me," she asked, "Is the silent song that people sing in their hearts the same as the songs the Yays sing in the Night Chant ?"

The boy answered, "I think it is the same song that everything sings. It is the song of the Turquoise Woman and the Bearer of the Day. It is the song of the Sky Father and the Earth Mother. It is the song that the rain sings to the corn, which answers it as it lies waiting in the ground."

His brother's wife leaned forward and put her little brown hand on Younger Brother's. She said, softly:

"It is the same song but only you know that."

As she spoke, Younger Brother was conscious of the old glid-ing sensation of his early dreams and he felt as he did when he lay on top of the Western Mountain, thinking of the Turquoise Woman. With conviction he said:

"It is the same song that the whole world is singing. I heard it when I made my offering to the wide water. I have heard the Star Children sing it at night while the Earth Mother slept."

"Little Singer," said the woman, "I have heard the stars sing in the daytime and I have listened to them many times while the Sun Bearer sang his daylight song."

Younger Brother gazed into the dark brown eyes with their far-away look and he said:

"You should be a medicine woman for you know hidden things and secrets deep in the heart of things."

"I know this much, Little Singer. There are secrets we can not name, songs we cannot hear, and words we must not speak."

"That is true," said the boy. "Uncle has told me that Heaven and Earth have four sons who made the first sand painting, but he says only medicine men may utter their names. Even I have not heard those sacred names."

The wife of Elder Brother smiled as she said:

"I could guess those names if I tried. I know what Mother Earth would name her sons, but I too must keep the secrets of the mothers."

She rose and picked up her can of pebbles to fling at the sheep grazing among the rocks. "Yego," she called as she drove her flock over the crest of the hill.

Younger Brother watched her red skirt swishing about her little feet as she disappeared behind the trees. He returned to his weeding, wondering if his brother's wife really did know the names of the four sons of Heaven and Earth.

After an hour of weeding in the hot sunshine, Younger Brother went back to his mother's hogan. She had her loom set under a summer shelter of cedar boughs. It was very restful there in the shade. His mother said to him:

"Are the watermelons growing ?"

"The plants are doing well. I have sheltered them from the wind with rocks."

"It will be good to have our melons. I am glad you are a farmer."

The boy looked pleased as he said:

"The young man who floated down the river in the hollow log was a farmer. He made the first garden and the Yays taught him how to cook the corn and squash. They told him he must not cook the watermelon because if he did, the Navahos would always cook them."

Mother looked up from her weaving and laughed. She said:

"Why, everyone knows that watermelons should not be cooked. I never even thought of such a thing."

"Did you ever think of eating raw squash ?" asked the boy.

"Of course not. That would be foolish. I should not like its taste."

"When you cook the squash, you always boil it in a pot with beans, don't you ?"

"Of course I do. Why do you ask such foolish questions ?"

"I was just thinking," said the boy, "how wise you are and how much you know. Uncle has told me that the Yays taught our people all the things you know."

"If Uncle says so, it is true of the ancient ones, but the Yays did not teach me how to cook beans and squash. I always knew how. My mother always knew how. But my mother taught me how to weave. That was difficult at first. The yarn would be tight in places and loose in places, and my mother would make me pull out the work I had done."

Younger Brother looked at the even, tight weaving on the loom and said:

"Your mother taught you how to weave the yarn in and out, in and out, until it was even and smooth, but who taught you how to make the patterns, which no one else makes ?"

"My patterns ?" asked Mother. "How can I say who taught me those ? They grow by themselves. When they are done, I say, 'Here is a cloud on a summer sky. Here is a star in a winter night.' "

Younger Brother drew close to his mother and said:

"Tell me the secret of where patterns come from. I want to know if they are like the song in my heart."

"My child," said the mother, "if I could answer that I would be wiser than Uncle. I am not wise in my head. I can only cook and spin and weave for my children. That is woman's work. Your father can work with silver. Your uncle can sing the songs that heal. You are a farmer. Do not ask me what makes your seeds grow. Neither ask me what makes my patterns grow. It is enough that they do."

The mother looked out toward the mesa where purple shadows were creeping slowly upward. She saw Little Sister coming home with the sheep.

"The child will be hungry," she said. "I must make the bread and coffee."

CHAPTER XXXIII

THE DEEP BELOW

AY AFTER DAY the Sun Bearer slanted his rays down to earth, while the corn and the beans reached upward.

Sometimes the lightning serpents struck their fire into the garden to warm the soil deep down. The soft rain moistened the ground and freshened the leaves. The garden of Younger Brother promised a full yielding.

The melons and squashes were set and the tassels showed on the corn.

"My garden grows fast," said the boy to his brother, who rode over one morning to visit. Elder Brother carried his rifle with him. He wanted to hunt.

"Get on your pony and come with me," he said to Younger Brother. "We will ride to the canyon for rabbits."

The little farmer was glad of a chance to go. He said:

"Wait till I saddle my horse. Shall I take the bow and arrow?"

"Take it if you want to. I like to shoot with a gun."

203

When the pony was ready, the two brothers rode gayly away in the fresh sage-scented air, gossiping as they rode.

"You know that Cut Finger who burned the store ?" said Elder Brother.

"Yes, I know that Cut Finger, that spittle of coyotes, that child of hunger.   What of him ?"

"He is in the calaboose of the Pelicanos."

"Let him stay there.   He is no good to Navahos."

"They say he sickens and is no good to Pelicanos either," said Elder Brother.

"Who told you about him ?"

"That policeman who caught him.   I saw him at the trading post of the Big Man."

"What does the Big Man say about it ?" asked Younger Brother.

"I only heard him say that if people had work to do, they wouldn't steal nor kill.   He believes in everyone keeping busy."

"So do I," said Younger Brother.   "With my weeding and hoeing and singing with Uncle, I have no time for killing."

Elder Brother laughed so loud his pony pricked up its ears and ran a little faster.   The pinto followed the lead.   Just as Younger Brother found himself rounding a curve in the trail, a jack rabbit jumped out from behind a bush.   In an instant the boy released the arrow in his bow and shot the animal.

Elder Brother jumped down to pick up the game.   He said:

"That was quick work.   It does not take much time for you to kill."

"When I hunt, I hunt," said the boy proudly.   He was just

as much surprised as his brother was, but he pretended to be very calm. He tied the rabbit to his saddle and they both rode on again.

Before noon the two were back home. Elder Brother had a prairie dog to take to his wife. Mother took care of the rabbit and said:

"The farmer is now a hunter. That is good. He will make a fine husband when he marries."

Uncle was at Mother's hogan and he said:

"Yes, if more Navahos were like him, none would go hungry."

Mother answered:

"My Elder Son is also a good hunter."

"That is true also. He and I have hunted together when we went to the forest for deer. He helped me to catch the one for the unwounded buckskin. When our men had surrounded the deer so that we could catch him, your Elder Son held him while I put the bag of pollen over his nose."

Younger Brother, listening, said:

"Some day I also will do that. When I climbed the Waterless Mountain with Uncle, we saw the land of our people spreading to east, to south, to west, to north. We saw in the distance the dark mountains where the deer hide. We saw the canyons where the Cactus People live among mirages. We saw the sky like a turquoise bowl above us. All these wonders we saw as we stood on top of the Waterless Mountain."

Uncle said:

"Yes, you and I together saw how far spreads the land of our people but I alone saw the Soft-footed Chief as he walked in beauty past the child of my sister."

Younger Brother answered:

"I saw his tracks near where I slept. I saw them when the light came in the eastern sky."

Mother, who had been listening, looked worried as she said:

"You never told me that the Soft-footed Chief walked past my Younger Son."

"There are some happenings we do not speak of," said Uncle. "It is better to be quiet until one understands. In the deep heart of things are many mysteries. Who knows what is hidden beneath the earth ?"

Mother said:

"There are enough things on top of the earth for me to think about. There are my sheep, there are the hills they feed upon, and there is my wool and my loom and my children and there is the water the Big Man brought down in the pipe."

"Yes," said Younger Brother, "there is the water which keeps our sheep alive. It flows on top of the earth where the sun shines upon it. You can see it, you can drink it, and you do not question its source."

"Why should I so long as it is there ? It is like my patterns in weaving. I do not know where they come from."

Uncle said:

"My sister, you have spoken truth. None of us knows what is at the heart of things."

"I know," said Younger Brother, "that Waterless Mountain

*I alone saw the Soft-footed Chief as he walked in beauty past
the child of my sister.*

hides a pool in its heart. I know that the water that gives life to our sheep comes from that pool."

The boy's face was so full of conviction that his mother could not doubt. She said to Uncle:

"Where does the child get his wisdom?"

Uncle looked very serious as he answered:

"Always the Pack Rat has guided him. I knew that the Pack Rat was wise about the east and north, the west and south, but I now think he knows about the above and the deep below. He must have taught our child."

CHAPTER XXXIV

CARRYING ON

HEEP shearing time had come and gone. The wool from the sheep's backs found itself packed into big gunny sacks. The Navahos had driven wagon loads of the hundred pound sacks to the trading post. There they had been weighed and paid for. Father and Mother had gone together to the post and brought back flour and sugar and coffee.

The difficult winter had passed and again the sheep had redeemed the pawn of their owners. Nearly all the Navahos were resplendent in their turquoise.

Corn was ripe enough to roast and some of the melons were ready to eat. Younger Brother felt the pride of a successful farmer. He rode to the trading post to deliver two watermelons to the Big Man. He went into the little room back of the store and handed to his friend a sack containing the melons.

"Here they are, Grandfather," he said with pride. "I have caused to grow many brothers and sisters of these melons. I wish to sell some of them."

"That should be easy, my boy. There is to be a girl dance near here next week. Bring in a load."

"If there is to be a dance, I think I shall go. I am a farmer now and old enough to join the men. Now I will return to my garden."

All the family prepared for the festival. They rode through the warm, clear air of evening and arrived at the dance ground about nine o'clock.

They added their wagon and horses to the circle surrounding two bands of Navahos singing to the accompaniment of the medicine man's pottery drum.

Younger Brother joined a group of young men and listened to the songs. He saw logs added to the campfire and watched the young wand-bearer come into the firelight and wave her wand.

He remembered how he had helped to dress a wand when he was a little boy. He thought how much he had learned since then of the ways of his people. He was feeling really grown-up, since he had become a farmer and produced food for the family. He felt like a man — like the rest of the men around him.

He was aware of a very big yellow moon rising behind the cedar trees. Then he was aware that a girl was pulling at his blanket. She wanted him to dance.

He was shy — really and truly shy — because he had never before danced with a girl. He did what she wished and found himself going slowly round and round in the firelight, while the girl held tightly to the back of his blanket.

He kept his blanket wrapped around him so that the girl

would not pull it off. His feet moved like all the feet, but he was sure that no one's heart beat as fast as his. He had strange new feelings.

He thought it must be the sound of the pottery drum, or the chorus of men's voices that made him feel so queer, or maybe it was the extraordinary size of the yellow moon, which came up slowly as if it, too, were keeping time to the drum.

Everything was timed. He knew that, but he thought his heart was out of time. It beat too fast. Whenever he became conscious of the girl's hand taking a tighter grip on his blanket, his heart beat out of time. His feet were all right. They shuffled along like all the other feet and turned him slowly round and round.

The moon rose higher. The firelight gleamed on the silver belts of the dancers and intensified the red of the blankets.

Everyone seemed to be going slowly round and round. That was right. Everything was right except his heart. He knew it beat too fast.

There were very many of his people sitting on the ground under the moonlight. Always they had done that. Years and hundreds of years back they had sat that way while the young men danced with the girls.

He could feel how the songs and the drumming were telling of his people — of their living, of their wars and of their victories. He could feel how the ground itself was part of his people, how the trees were part of them, and how the Moon Bearer was one of them.

The Moon Bearer was a very old one of his people, and he carried the moon because he liked its beauty.

This girl, who held so tightly to his blanket -- she was like the moon when it is young. He would like to be the bearer of a young moon.

When he thought that, his heart gave a great thump. It seemed as if he could hear its beat above the drum, and then he could feel the blood coursing through his veins, warming his body and making him conscious of all the men and women and children about him, whose veins carried the same blood as his.

His heart sang a new song. It was a song of his people who had lived in the land when the Ancients dwelt in the cliffs — his people, who had hungered and fought and made songs as they carried on — his people, who could sing — mothers who could weave — uncles who could heal — children, who laughed — and young men and girls, who could dance in the moonlight.

The little hand at his back clasped his blanket more tightly, and he knew that a new song was being born in his heart. It was the song of his people, who carried on, who persisted, who danced to the throbbing music of their hearts.

At last he understood the pain of beauty that he had felt on top of the western mountain. He remembered how he had wondered if there were anyone in the world who felt as he felt.

Now he knew that all of his people felt as he felt. Had not the little pottery drums been telling the secret in the moonlight for thousands of years?

As the pale light in the eastern sky foretold the coming of the sun, the drum ceased its throbbing and the men's voices were stilled. The girls returned to their mothers.

Younger Brother greeted the east with a consciousness of new power rising within him.

Dawn Boy was making way for the Bearer of the Day.